THE RACE

A NOVELLA

JACKE WILSON

To my family, for filling life with enthusiasm

ACKNOWLEDGMENTS

Many thanks to my earliest readers and strongest supporters: Ronica, Charlie, Mike, Michael, Ronica's mom, Keith, Jan, and above all Jee Yoon.

I would also like to thank Emily Nemchick for her excellent editing work. Any errors are, sadly, my own.

ONE

THROUGHOUT THE CAMPAIGN, REPORTERS asked me why the Governor was running. Not if I thought he'd win or what he'd do once elected, but *why*. Why's he running? Why? Why? Why's he doing this to *us*? Why's he doing this to *himself*?

I never knew how to answer. He was a career politician, one of those creatures who need validation by an electorate the way athletes need competition or businessmen need to make money. An egomaniac, a narcissist, a damaged personality looking to fill some kind of hole—all the usual explanations were obvious and true. Only it was not enough for them. Not this time.

I'd usually mumble something or other I'd heard the Governor say—that he wanted to help others, that he believed he was the best person to represent the good people of Wisconsin. But it was no good: they knew I was not a true believer. I'd been on the scene for weeks, not years. I was not a chief of staff or a whispering guru or a speechwriter or a handler or any kind of political advisor. I wasn't even a member of his party. Not a relative, not a friend. I was just there.

"Is this another one of your strays?" my wife asked

1

when I told her I was taking a few months off to work on the autobiography of a man nobody loved. "Governor Olson? The 'gone snowmobiling' guy?"

"That's the one."

She sighed. "Another stray."

"It's a paying job," I said.

She knew, even then, that I would become more deeply involved than the project required. She knew this even though she had no idea that the Governor was planning to run again. None of us did.

Why?

I suppose what follows is my attempt to answer the question:

Why did he run?

And another of my own:

Why do we care?

EVEN BEFORE I RECEIVED THE MATERIALS I had been tracking the Governor's career. There was not much else in our town to be excited about. Anyone who broke out of the parochial limits of our area gained the notice, the respect, and the appreciation of everyone in the community. A golfer from a nearby town turned pro and stayed on the Masters leaderboard until late Sunday afternoon: *Yes! We're still here! We exist!* Our town produced a tug-of-war team that competed in the World Championships in Ireland: *Yes! Third in the entire world! We matter now! We count!*

And now…a governor with national aspirations. From a town not far from ours.

Even so, I was astonished to receive the box. Why me? I had an MFA, which made me a writer, purportedly, and a law degree, which meant I could call myself a lawyer—but I was not a politician or a journalist, let alone a biographer. Was this a mistake? A prank?

The package contained two manuscript boxes, six or seven hundred pages of material. There was no cover letter.

He called later that day.

"It's my autobiography," he explained. "I need some help with the organization. I'm a busy man. When can you start?"

"I'm busy too," I said.

"I'll pay you," he said, brushing off my reluctance. "You'll enjoy it. I've had a *fascinating* life."

He assumed I would agree—but then again, he could. Any reporter in the country would have taken his call; he could have appeared on any talk show he wanted. Even minor scandals have a way of giving you that power. And his scandal had been spectacular.

It's easy to forget now just how incredible it all was. A sitting governor, an incipient national campaign. Getting traction in the primaries. Not likely to win, but a press favorite. A good chance at being on the presidential ticket.

And then: a disappearance. His staff is cagey. Their first story is that he's in bed with a cold. Then they say he's "up north snowmobiling." The catch phrase takes off: *Saturday Night Live* bases a skit on it. Rumors abound: rehab, depression, marital problems. Someone says they saw him at an airport. Finally the staff admits they aren't sure where he is. The governor! Of the state! Is gone!

That was the story for a few wondrous days. The truth when it emerged was just as surprising. He'd gone off, leaving everyone behind—his wife, his four kids, his campaign, *the state he was in charge of*—all to go and visit his mistress in Italy.

That, of course, was the first big *why*.

True love? That's what he claimed in public.

It's never that simple.

I read enough in the pages he'd sent me to see that there was a more complicated answer.

I took the job to find out what it was.

HE WANTED ME TO MEET HIM at the Big Boy restaurant on Highway 14, near I-90. It was a restaurant I did not know still existed. Not just their Janesville location, but the entire Big Boy franchise. Who still ate there? How did they keep going? But there it was, still chugging away. I sat down on a bench in the lobby and watched Wisconsinites come and go.

After a few minutes a boy came in—he was maybe four or five—ahead of whoever had brought him.

"There he is!" he shouted, and came running toward me.

I stood up, my mind making all kinds of leaps. This boy must be a grandson. The grownups must have told the little boy that they were on their way to meet someone important, a writer who was going to be helping Grampa with an important project.

My mind put all this together in a second, and it changed everything. I stood up, flattered, determined to live up to their expectations. I was a writer, in their eyes if no one else's, significant enough to make this little guy thrilled to meet me.

I bent over, ready to give him a high five. The boy ran past me and flung his arms around the statue I'd been sitting next to.

"Oh, Big Boy!" he cried. "I *knew* you'd still be here!"

And Big Boy, the chubby, wavy-haired, smiling lad with the red suspenders and tablecloth overalls and big cherub cheeks and blank eyes, stood in place, absorbing the hug. He was, indeed, still there.

I straightened up and smiled at the mother trailing behind, who stared at me and frowned. Then I drifted into the restaurant.

The Governor was already seated, eating a piece of pie.

He had ordered one for me too, but when I didn't turn

up in time he went ahead and ate both. "Sorry about that," he said with a chuckle. "It's too good. Too, too good!"

If he was embarrassed—some would say that a failure to control his impulses was not anything he should be laughing about—he did not let it show.

It was strange to see him in reduced circumstances, not quite unrecognized by the people here, but overlooked. He was wearing a sportcoat and tie, and he still had the shine of a politician: hair blow-dried and tamed by product, big white teeth, a bronzy glow to his skin. I could see why the press had viewed him as nationally viable: he was conventionally, if blandly, handsome. If he'd become president he'd have been one of the thinner ones, and one of the more distinguished-looking: a fresh, youthful look, with smooth grooves of worry lines. It was a versatile face: wise and caring, rugged in times of war, sleek and inoffensive in times of peace. For some reason he made me think of a ten-dollar bill: reliable but easily forgotten.

As is often the case when I encounter people like him, I felt like I was supposed to feel some kind of excitement, but I did not. This was a man who'd held power, whose career and life had been blown apart by a sensational scandal, and who even now had a tabloid-cover international celebrity that was only months old. You might think there would be some buzz around him, but I felt nothing. I felt no *aura*.

And yet, he carried himself as if he had it. He was brimming with self-confidence, and self-esteem. It was like a doctor who acts like a doctor even outside the hospital— on the golf course, say, even though his status at the hospital doesn't matter there.

The waitress came by and his political side emerged. "That pie was *absolutely delicious*," he said, beaming. "So good I wish I could eat another."

She was bored and tired, but she treated him with affection, smiling just for him, as if he alone among all her customers could make her day.

"Looks like you already had two," she said, loading the plates onto her tray.

"These *must* be Wisconsin cherries!"

"You know it, doll," she said, bustling away.

It was a fascinating exchange. In fact the pie had been filled with a gelatinous cherry-like substance that had probably come from some factory in New Jersey.

"Let's talk about the book!" he said to me. "You've read it?"

I nodded.

"Couldn't put it down, right? It's got everything in it. It's all there," he said. "It could use some organization. Maybe some rearranging—you can help with that. Some chapters are too long. We could break 'em in two, you know. People are busy, they like short chapters."

I nodded again. The book had a lot more trouble than he seemed to realize. It was, in fact, a complete mess.

"A couple times I felt like I said the same thing twice. And there might be a spot or two where it runs out of steam. You can help me fill those in."

"Sure."

He nodded more to himself than to me. "It's got no ending, I know, but guess what?" He put both hands on the edge of the table, leaned forward, and lowered his voice. "My story is not over."

I didn't know what he meant. Of course he had many years still ahead of him, and he had a chance to live them with some measure of dignity. I imagined him working as a lawyer, or a lobbyist, in a low-profile, behind-the-scenes way. He had plenty of businessman friends. He could put his marriage back together, eventually, and serve on boards and blue-ribbon committees assessing budgets or job-creation programs. He could move to D.C. or stay in Wisconsin, and work hard. In twenty years he'd be a "whatever happened to..." guy and people would be impressed that he was still around and had not continued to embarrass himself.

But this was not what he had in mind. His eyes were wide open and dancing. They were blue, as infinite and as thin as the sky, wide but not deep.

"I'm running for Congress," he said, as a slow grin took over his face. He leaned back in the booth and pounded the table with his palms. "We'll give this book a heck of a last chapter!"

I mumbled some kind of agreement. I think I also mentioned—incredibly, it seems to me now—that the book probably didn't need a new ending if he decided to change his mind. Why did I say that? Why do you tell someone to stop downing shots of tequila? Concern for humiliation, poor judgment, maybe physical well-being. It was a human instinct.

But he was determined. "Let's go see Tina!" he said, dropping money on the table and loping toward the door.

That was all I needed. If you care about my motivation—me, a nobody—then that was it. That was my why. This narrative was rushing forward and I couldn't turn away.

Tina Olson? The wife who had called him "a fifth-rate husband, a shoddy human being, and a washed-up Judas"? And not only would I get to witness their encounter, I would be driving the car that took him there? I did think we'd get a new ending for his book, but maybe not the one he expected.

On the way out he made sure to swing by the cash register and tell the manager how great the service had been. The waitress appeared, and the Governor immediately fished another bill out of his wallet. It was a ten.

"An *extra* tip," he said, bestowing it on her. "Never had a better time."

The woman beamed.

It was in him to be a politician. He had all the skills, and the energy, and the spirit.

And now, headed to see his wife? He would need it.

TWO

IF THE GOVERNOR WAS NERVOUS he didn't show it. He was so relaxed I thought he must have had some inside information. Some news passed along, some reason to think things would go smoothly. I had not yet learned that he didn't need one.

I was completely pulled in: as we drove down Milton Avenue and out toward the river I was looking forward to seeing the encounter, though I thought it might be awkward for me as well as for the Governor. What would I say, where would I stand, what would I do with my hands?

Janesville had not changed much in the past twenty years. We reached a wealthy neighborhood that looked unfamiliar until I realized that it was just updated with a handful of new homes and some greener landscaping. It had the same old feel: this was where rich people set themselves apart from the rest of us.

Success in a small world is different, better in some ways, worse in others. And this, what the Governor had, was broken success. You could see that immediately as we pulled into the driveway. He owned this house. It was a nice house but not a happy one.

I was more impressed by Tina. Everyone was. She was

younger than him, in the prime of her life. Competent, powerful, and beautiful, with perfect hair and just the right amount of makeup, her face richly mature but not old. She'd have been a dynamite First Lady, as attractive as any we've had.

And one of the most capable. As the only daughter of a doting father, the founder and sole owner of a massively successful company that made medical supplies, she had spent her twenties and most of her thirties running his business and running it well. She had also raised four boys and had been a popular First Lady of the state. She'd been an active member of the Governor's political team while remaining above the fray, untainted by politics. *Vote for him and get the pair* was a common refrain throughout his first campaign. *She should run* was common in his second.

Now it was *that poor thing*, a role she did not want to play. She had not stuck with the Governor during the scandal. She'd been angry and hurt and had left him to twist in the wind of the extremely awkward press conferences, alone, without her. She had refused to stand next to him with that creepy, hostage-like smile on her face.

"Who's he?" Tina said to the Governor in the foyer.

"My biographer!"

I explained that it was actually an autobiography—I was just helping him do some organization.

"Don't sell yourself short!" the Governor said, gripping my shoulder.

I had not intended this comment to be self-deprecating—in fact it was something of the opposite. I wanted her to know that *he* had been writing his memoirs, that he was paying me…not that I was so drawn to his story that I, on my own initiative…I was not a vulture looking to feast on their marital carcass…but at that moment one of his boys crossed through the room and the Governor chased after him down the hallway.

Tina clearly didn't know what to do with me. I had no options but to stand there. Finally she invited me into the living room where we did not sit down but ventured into small talk.

It surprised me that she recognized my last name.

"Are you Mandy's brother?"

"She's a second cousin," I said.

"And you live in D.C. now? What do you do there?"

I saw a flicker of approval, or at least curiosity. I was one of the ones who had left. Yet I was not such a success that she'd heard of me. I told her I was basically a lawyer.

"Basically?" She smiled faintly.

"I guess I am one," I said. "It's not something I ever thought I'd be."

"A long story?"

I nodded.

She looked down the hallway. Now I saw her full smile; it dazzled me. "We've got time," she said with a shrug.

"It's strange," I began, "to feel, every minute of every day, that you're only pretending to be something that you're not. I went to law school, I'm a member of the bar, I get paid to do the tasks that lawyers do. I meet with clients, go to court, confer with judges—and yet I never feel like it's me doing these things. It's not what I feel like I really am."

She smiled warmly. "And what do you feel like you really are?"

"A failure," I said.

For a moment it appeared as though she might laugh, but just then the Governor returned and I was forgotten. Her mouth hardened, her eyes narrowed; she looked young and desperate to be rid of this old man who had trapped her in something she hadn't expected.

He noticed none of this. "Luke's doing great!" he said. "He's thinking about heading to Madison for college. The UW!"

"I'd like him to go out of state," she said.

"He'll do great no matter *where* he goes," said the Governor with a huge smile.

I feel compelled to explain here that I'd spent the past few days immersed in hundreds of pages of the Governor's thoughts, much of it covering experiences he and Tina had shared and his feelings about the two of them.

What had I learned? I knew he had an unrelenting optimism, a switch constantly flipped on, a dial cranked to one side and taped in place. Maximum optimism. I also knew that he had believed to his core that Tina was his perfect counterpart. They'd been young and in love, raising four kids. He regretted what he'd done to her.

That was implied, anyway. It was *my* interpretation if not explicitly his. One of my notes was that he should go at this more directly.

He had plenty of chances to do so. The story of *her* finding out—not the exposure by the press, but the moment *Tina* found out, was something he circled back to again and again. All his future, all his past, had collapsed into that instant. It was a riveting moment, to be sure—but as things currently stood it was a significant problem for the book I was supposed to help him shape. Every childhood story, every young-man-in-love story, every political event—everything before or since led to a discussion of that moment. The moment when Tina had learned the truth, and his days as a husband and parent and upstanding member of the community had ended. A new life had begun. The presence of this moment, the constant return to it, grew repetitive and tiresome. Worse, it undercut his trustworthiness as a narrator. Clearly he was obsessed with this moment, but he was incapable of facing it directly.

This was a problem the book's structure, which I now realized was a problem in his life as well. I was essentially a stranger, newly introduced to her and to him not much longer before, and yet I knew intimate details known to no other person in the world. I knew about their courtship, their first sexual experiences, their private conversations about love and marriage and parenting. I knew about the miscarriage that they'd never made public. I knew that, as a young executive, she'd had to fire a stepbrother for drug addiction, and how she'd kept this out of the press in order to help him put his life back together (which he'd done). I knew funny stories, details about the sex they'd had on their honeymoon (an airplane bathroom, quite explicit and funny and unforgettable). Their ambitions and fears and hopes and dreams—all that was known to me.

But there was more: I knew how much this encounter meant to the Governor. I knew there was something deep within him that needed her to approve of his decision. She may have known it too. But she could not give it to him. I could see it on her face as he asked her to sit down and listen to a new proposal, and as she reluctantly sat across from the man she despised (with me, the unlikely witness lurking in the corner). Maybe it was spite, and maybe it was just sheer astonishment. Hadn't she given enough? Hadn't he taken more than his share? He had *destroyed* her present, and her future, and her past.

"You probably want to know why I'm here," he began.

"I had hoped it was to see your kids."

"That too! Of course!" he said. "Always love doing that, *every* chance I get. But there's something else."

"A change in the custody arrangement?"

"No…no, that's fine. That's for the lawyers. No offense," he said to me.

"None taken," I croaked.

"Tina," said the Governor. "There's a seat coming open. The First District. Lyle Larson's retiring."

"So?"

"I can win it, Tina. U.S. Congress."

"Oh God."

"It's a wide-open field. I'll enter as the front runner."

I thought Tina might faint. She put her head between her knees and remained there, bent over, for at least a minute.

The Governor must have seen this before. He smiled patiently, occasionally tilting his head back and forth in a not-much-longer gesture, until finally she reemerged, her face red and slowly draining as she took deep breaths.

"We can do it," the Governor said with a campaign smile.

"Are you *insane?*"

"You could win it too," said the Governor. "If you run, I'm out. I'd never interfere with that…I hope you know that….Are you interested?"

She looked at him, still stunned. "This isn't happening."

"You let me know. But before the deadline, which is tomorrow. I wanted to let you know I'm filing. I came here to get your blessing."

"You don't have it."

The Governor barked a laugh and looked at me because he needed someone to share this with. I smiled weakly. I was still standing. My hands were somewhere or other.

"Well, okay, *blessing* isn't the right word," he said to Tina. His face turned serious again. "I just need to know you're not opposed."

"I am opposed," she said. "One thousand percent opposed."

He laughed again, harder than before, in a *what will she say next* way. He looked at me, shaking his head. *This is why I married her. Isn't she hilarious?* This time I did not smile.

He cleared his throat. "Now, there's opposed, like in your heart, and opposed, like you try to obstruct. Like for the latter, maybe you'd give an interview, or—God forbid—endorse one of the other candidates."

She stared at him.

"The people love you, Tina, they always have."

She said nothing.

I was riveted. This was flattery, maybe. Maybe it was a way to express *his* love.

She cut him off. Her face was not as red as before, but she looked alive, engaged, *present*. Her eyes were bright and flashing.

"You are the father of my children," she said in a tone that made my skin tingle. "I will not criticize their father in a way that hurts them. For their sake I will not participate in the kind of public humiliation that you evidently feel compelled to inflict upon yourself. You should disappear, Tom. You should hide under a rock submerged in a lake in the middle of a country no one has ever heard of. Run for Congress? You should refrain from ever showing your duplicitous face in this state again. Opposed? Every time I see you on television or see your photo in a magazine it kills me. The memory of who I thought you were has been *ruined* by the knowledge of who you are. And it's not just what you did to me, Tom. It's what you did to a lot of good people. Your supporters. Your staff. People who believed in you…

"And I, who loved you. Who shared your bed, who bore your children. I, who financed your first campaign. I stood by you through everything—until you forced me to live through what no woman should ever have to endure. When you ran for office I gave up everything to help run your campaign. For nothing. Nothing but *you*, Tom, *your* goals, *your* dreams. Have you forgotten? Does it mean nothing? Does it not count? Do *I* not matter to you?"

She took a breath.

"I gave up so much for you, Tom. And it's gone. And now I live with pain and humiliation that I share with no one. Who could understand what it means to be your wife, to have gone through the public shame you imposed on me?

"I will suffer in silence if that's what my sons need. But if you need some kind of redemption, a return to your past, you will do that with my silence and suffering. You will be contributing to my pain. I am barely alive, Tom. I'm lying in a grave that you dug, that you shoved me into.

Now you're back—why? To extend a hand? Of course not. You're here to whack my head with a shovel and tell me that soon you'll be heaping more dirt on my body. And..."

She trailed off. There was nothing left to say.

The Governor took all this in. He paused to make sure she was finished.

The grandfather clock in the foyer ticked. In the quiet room it sounded like a sledgehammer slamming down on an iron spike.

At last the Governor smiled. "You could run my campaign," he said. "You'd be absolutely fantastic at that. I could pay you this time!"

He smiled in a way that denied the possibility that anyone could truly hate him. It was not arrogant and it was not entirely oblivious. He was just trying to see the positives here, that's all...

Tina was not joining him on the sunny side of the street. She was still in her grave.

"Get...the...*hell*...out of my house."

She was not a woman who swore often; the *hell* carried a lot of weight.

We said some quick goodbyes that were not returned. The door slammed behind us; two deadbolts hammered shut.

We walked to the driveway and got in the car—it was strange again to see the Governor next to me, in the passenger seat of the car I'd rented. I drove around the circular driveway and back down to the gate, waiting for the Governor to say something.

He drummed his fingers on his leg, hummed a little as we turned onto the road and passed along the fence that lined his property, picking up speed.

You would not know he had just been on the receiving end of a furious cannon blast of a speech. You would think he was a guy who'd just won a minor lottery, a hundred bucks on a scratch-off, say, and who was on his way to play some golf with a few buddies before coming home to mow the lawn, which he didn't mind doing on a cool evening.

I listened to him hum, trying to figure out the tune. It sounded like something from a Disney movie.

Finally, as we reached the main road, he spoke.

"Probably best to keep that one out of the book," he said with a chuckle.

THREE

AFTER THE MEETING WITH TINA I returned to D.C. for a few days to catch up with my family. It didn't go all that well—everyone was doing fine without me, and my wife knew my mind was still in Wisconsin.

"Go back," she said. "Go back to your strays."

"There's a Sunday flight," I said. "But I could stay through Monday morning and—"

"Go. Go. Go."

On Saturday night we had dinner with our friends the Biltons. Ross was from Nottingham, Erin was from Sydney, and now they both worked in D.C. for world financial institutions. My wife and I have moved frequently, and over time we've noticed—it's happened too often to be coincidental—that our best friends always seem to be European, Asian, something foreign, or, in a pinch, Canadian. Not Americans, I guess is the point. I have no idea why. I can drill down into motives but none of them seem quite right. We hate our country? We hate ourselves? No. It's something else, I think: we don't fit into any sub-categories. We're American, broadly, but that's as granular as we want to be. No other groups will have us.

Practically speaking, this honed my skills at explaining

things about America in a high school civics class kind of way. I was not a specialist, but a generalist. I hated debating particular clauses of the Constitution with other Americans, but I enjoyed explaining its basic structure or function in a big-picture way. I could give a dime-store version of why the jury system was more reflective of American values than the judicial inquiries of the civil law system.

That Saturday night my wife was eager to tell them about the Governor.

"You *have* to let me tell them. It's the only thing you do that's not confidential."

I waved my hand for her to continue. She began with the box of papers, the phone call, and the negotiation.

"So he—well, he can't just take a leave of absence, can he? He has partners to consider. They rule him. So he has a meeting with the management committee, persuades them of the importance of this. They agree. They work out the compensation issues, the time he'll spend away. It's all very formalized. I've seen calendars. I've seen spreadsheets."

"Impressive," said Erin, smiling at me. "I had no idea you were so important."

I smiled vaguely. I was being a good sport.

"He needed a number. The number! How much he'd do this for. This governor has money, you know, his wife is like the snap-on-tools heiress or something. And anyway the campaign–" She turned to me. "The campaign *is* paying for this, right?"

"Probably."

"That's right, you don't know, because you haven't been paid yet. We'll see....So anyway he comes up with his number. Fifty bucks an hour. Fifty. Gotta get fifty bucks an hour. That's the bare minimum my husband decides he's worth. Fifty."

"It seemed like a fair price," I said.

Erin could see this was headed somewhere embarrassing. "Oh no."

"Not just *fair*," said my wife. "'This is what we do in Wisconsin,' my husband said. 'We set our price and state it for the record. There will be no haggling. A man names his price. Another man agrees to pay it. We stand on equal ground.' So says my husband."

"Oh dear," Erin said.

"So he's on the phone, and this is what I hear: 'Right. Well, I'm glad you asked. My fee for this is fifty dollars an hour….Okay, great. See you Thursday.' And he hangs up the phone. So I'm pretty impressed, right? I say, wow, that was easy, you named your price and he agreed. And my husband looks at me and says, 'No.'"

"No?" Erin asked.

"He says, 'No. No, he didn't.' Because the Governor didn't agree! The great Wisconsin non-haggle. Name your price and *immediately* agree to something lower!"

"Oh *dear*," said Erin, trying not to hurt my feelings. "But…you're a lawyer."

"Not a good one," I said.

"He was *trained* in negotiation!" my wife said. "Negotiation workshop! Two semesters!"

"Don't you negotiate deals all day long?" Erin asked.

"I'm a litigator," I said. "Not corporate. We don't really do deals."

Ross frowned. "Don't you negotiate settlements?"

I was at a loss. "Good point," I said.

"I know how to answer that," said my wife. "He has no clients!"

Everyone laughed at me. I smiled across the table. She is the love of my life.

The truth was much simpler. I had proposed fifty dollars an hour. "How's forty-eight fifty?" the Governor had replied.

What could I do then? Split the difference? I couldn't do the math that quickly. I chalked it up to learning something about his character: he was not my father. The Governor came from Wisconsin but was not one of the farmers or teachers or cops or factory workers I'd known. He was bourgeois and I was proletariat. Why don't we use those words anymore? Too loaded with history? In their simple meanings they are useful. One guy has money and acts a certain way, has a certain comfort with it. Others don't and have a different way of dealing with one another. *How's forty-eight fifty?* is a kind of reflexive bitch slap my father would never have considered doing; if someone had done it to him, he'd have walked away and not thought twice about it.

And yet: my father had no money and would have paid fifty. The Governor was rich and got a deal. My father needed money and yet he stood on principle. I did not need it as much and yet I took the job.

This was the difference: in the Governor's world, people respected him for his assertiveness. In my father's world, that kind of chiseling was viewed as the work of an asshole. I took no position. The worlds were different. That was all. Is New York better than California? They're different.

While I was pondering this, my wife had been telling Ross and Erin about the Governor. They remembered him now: the scandal was not that old and had not yet faded in memory.

"He just disappeared!" Ross said. "Even his staff didn't know where he'd got to!"

I said something like the Governor was a fascinating guy and that the scandal had a depth to it that had not yet been explored. I sensed the room had doubters. Erin asked if he wasn't just another politician "whose dick had gotten him in trouble."

I tried to explain what I meant. That it was not his genitals but his heart. At the press conference, for example, where he teared up and spoke so freely about the love he felt—the blinding love for Ludovica Lambertucci, the Italian mistress.

Some of the details were impossible to ignore. How he,

trying to save his marriage, but feeling the pull of true love in Italy, went on chaperoned dates with Ludovica Lambertucci in Chicago. He did this knowing he was giving up a chance at the presidency—his heart drove him to it, he said, and I believed him, sort of, because otherwise why would he bring along his wife's sister, who sent back reports that the two lovers remained chaste? That may not have been love, but it wasn't purely lust either. His wife wasn't bullied. She was tough, not someone to be pitied. This was not a typical scandal.

And he was not a typical guy. I had learned this from the memoirs. He had something of the nineteenth century about him. He built his father's coffin, for example, using trees from their land that he himself chopped, planed, and sanded by hand. After the scandal he retreated up north to his family's cabin, where he grew a beard. He started his memoirs. Now he was clean-shaven and running again.

What else was there? The nevers.

The Governor had never drunk alcohol. Never tried coffee. Had never used a "cuss word." But there was more. He had never tried pizza. Or rice. He had not flown in a plane until he was fifty.

"Is he Mormon?" Erin asked.

I said he wasn't, that he was Christian, but he struck me as more of a Buddhist in temperament. A Mormon living according to a code would not be all that interesting. A lapsed Mormon would be a familiar story, even a cliché. But *his* nevers—never eaten pasta, had never eaten any food with "sauce"—were not connected to religion. Self-discipline? Self-denial? It was not that either.

"Why's he running?" Ross and Erin asked.

I shrugged and said I did not know.

THE NEXT MORNING I RETURNED to Wisconsin. And that day it became clear, suddenly, that the Governor could lose. Another candidate emerged: a Wisconsin hero, a businessman who'd saved some popular resorts up north that had been threatening to relocate to Northern California. Tony Spanbauer had unlimited funds, a high name recognition, and a record unblemished by electoral politics.

I was there when the news reached the Governor. He was heartbroken.

"The deadline has passed," he said. "My party has ignored its own rules."

He did not seem to have thought this was possible. It struck me as naïve for a career politician.

"You could challenge it," I said.

"They must think they've found a loophole," he said, not listening to me. "They're wrong about that."

The party leaders had not even talked about a loophole. They'd just said they couldn't let the "national embarrassment that is Tom Olson" be the face of the party.

"You could take it to court," I said.

He looked at me, startled.

"What else can you do?" I said. "Withdraw?"

"Why would I do that?"

I mumbled something about Tony Spanbauer serving the public interest.

"So can I," said the Governor. "That's why I'm doing this."

What I didn't say was what everyone knew: Tony Spanbauer was critical of the Governor and it worked. The Governor's numbers tanked overnight. His own party didn't want anything to do with him. He went from being a distraction to being an unloved joke.

The weeks leading to the primary were painful. The Governor tried running on issues. Interviewers asked about Tina, and the Italian lover, and snowmobiling. He was shown the *Saturday Night Live* skit and asked, humiliatingly, if he thought someone who was a "national clown" could effectively represent Wisconsin.

"Absolutely," he said with that empty smile he sometimes wore. "I'll be proud to serve in that capacity."

His interviewer, a news anchor on a Milwaukee affiliate, wasn't finished. "Putting aside Wisconsin," she said, "is this good for *you*?"

Another vapid smile. "Of course it is," he said.

It was an odd question. What was behind it? Concern for him? For his wife and kids? Or did she think he'd gone off the rails—that only a masochist would run again, and set himself up for all the laughing and mocking and condescension (from people like herself!).

Even the *Wall Street Journal*, which for years had been his champion, abandoned him. They ran a political cartoon, a simple drawing of a cemetery above the caption "Political Career of Tom Olson." In the foreground stood a single tombstone, with the years the Governor had served and an epitaph:

"Up North Snowmobiling."

THE GOVERNOR DID NOT LOSE HOPE. Tony Spanbauer had agreed to one debate, the final Friday before the Tuesday election. The Governor and I arrived early and were escorted to the green room of a local TV studio. I looked at photos—Mike Holmgren! Herb Kohl!—while the Governor prepared from notes he'd written in longhand on yellow-lined paper he kept in a Bible.

He had no staff, just me. And I didn't know how to help him prepare, not that he needed much help. His political skills were razor sharp—he'd have been elected handily had it not been for the scandal. He was younger, brighter, more capable, and more experienced. His knowledge of the issues dwarfed those of Tony Spanbauer, who'd been a successful businessman but who was a political novice, relying on a few general ideas and a handful of zippy one-liners making fun of the Governor.

"I don't underestimate him," the Governor said. "He sticks to his message."

There was no criticism in this, and no self-pity. I was

surprised by the lack of self-awareness.

"What if he asks about Italy?" I asked.

"I hope he does. He can stick to what's irrelevant, and I'll talk about what's important."

I nodded. "The issues."

"No," he said seriously. "My heart."

No one came to get us. Five minutes before the scheduled start time we walked through the corridor and into the studio itself. Cameras were set up, and lights. I sat in one of the fifty or so seats behind the moderator's desk. The Governor went to the podium and opened his Bible.

What happened next was surreal. Tony Spanbauer never showed up. A producer finally came in and told us that the debate had been postponed indefinitely.

Two minutes later an audience member got the news on her phone. Spanbauer had suffered a heart attack on the way to the studio. He had been driven straight to the hospital.

Six hours later, we learned that he was dead.

THE PRIMARY WAS HELD THAT TUESDAY, but no one was thinking much about it. On Wednesday the Governor and I drove to Wisconsin Rapids, Tony Spanbauer's hometown. On the way the Governor told me he had offered to give a speech at the funeral, even though the family had not asked him to—in fact, they had asked him not to attend.

It was the first I'd heard that he was unwelcome there. We were crashing the funeral.

"Are you sure this is a good idea?" I asked.

He smiled. "I've been in politics a long time. There are no good ideas."

I expressed my surprise by the nihilism of this, which was atypical for the Governor.

"There are only *great* ones," he said, slapping the dashboard, delighted that he had tricked me.

I thought about the snowmobiling incident and whether that, in retrospect, could be considered great in any way. But I stayed silent. It took an unusual person to say a thing like that: watching this guy was turning into one of the more bizarre things I'd ever witnessed. I dreaded the funeral but also was kind of giddy about it, too.

The Swedberg & Swedberg-Schwarz Funeral Home was clean, airy, and bright, with a beautiful honey-colored wooden ceiling. There are some things Wisconsin does as well as any state. There was no deep history here. There was land, and forest, and fresh starts. Not a bad vibe for a funeral home, where mourners had to start the long, slow process of turning away from the past and toward the future.

We stood in line to pass by the casket and pay our respects. The Governor was noticed immediately. The widow stared at us with hate. The children, who were themselves the Governor's age, huddled together. No one shook hands with us. After we'd walked by the casket one of the sons pulled me aside.

"Get him out of here," he said.

"He wants to pay his respects."

"He's done that. Now go."

The Governor insisted on staying, of course. And when the minister asked if anyone had words or stories to share, he was the first to stand.

"I have a little something to say," he began.

I wish I could recreate the speech—I've tried several times to get this right. On the page the words aren't much, but they were appropriate and heartfelt, and the Governor was sincere and generous in his praise for Tony. It was not about the race at all, but a tribute to his life and the many good things he'd done. The many people he'd touched and inspired.

I was impressed, both by what he said and how he said it, and I guess I was also impressed by the complete lack of any kind of response by anyone in the audience. No one cried or nodded or did anything. Then I realized: no one was looking at the Governor. Every single person in the audience was looking at Tony's widow. Who was livid.

After the Governor brought his speech to a close, with a request for everyone to bow their heads in prayer, which no one did, the widow stood up.

"You are a *snake*," she said, raising an index finger and pointing at the Governor. "An evil, poisonous serpent. Tony hated you. He hated everything about you. He hated what you did to Tina. He thought it was a disgrace, a shame for our state to have a governor like you. And he had to run. We watched you in the news, acting like nothing had ever happened, and he turned to me. He was *choking* with anger. I thought he was having a heart attack *then*. 'I have to beat that son of a bitch,' he said.

"And it killed him. Running killed him—no, that wasn't it. His hate for you killed him. *You killed him.* We didn't want you here, we told you that, and you came anyway. Can't you do something that's not about you?"

The Governor stood up again. He smiled gently. "In times of grief, we don't always know what to say…"

"I know what to say!" the widow cried. "*Go to hell!*"

He nodded sadly. I was relieved when we finally left. Once again I felt like I'd been blasted in the chest, and I had not even been the direct target. My hands were trembling as I started up the car.

The Governor was unperturbed. He turned on the radio as we were pulling out of the parking lot. At that very moment, the local NPR station was announcing that Governor Tom Olson had just won the primary.

The Governor folded a stick of gum into his mouth, shaking his head at his good fortune. "Do you believe in signs?" he asked.

I didn't answer for a while. I was thinking about dumb luck that didn't always happen to the deserving.

After a few miles on the highway we pulled off to stop at a Tastee Freeze. The Governor ordered a cheeseburger with ketchup and pickles and an ice cream cone with sprinkles.

"Signs from who?" I said finally. "The people? God?"

The Governor looked serious. "It's not for me to say," he said, wiping ketchup from his mouth with a napkin. "I just try to stay humble. And do my best."

Then he pulled out his cell phone and called his Italian lover.

FOUR

I FREELY CONFESS THAT I SPEND too much time think-ing about the Beatles. I don't have many heroes, but they come the closest.

Which is why it pained me so much when two things happened several years ago:

1) Yoko claimed that Paul was the Salieri to John's Mozart, condemned to misery and frustration by his prox-imity to the greater artist, and

2) Paul tried to get the Lennon-McCartney credits changed to McCartney-Lennon for several of the songs they (or he) had written.

For days I wrestled with the news as they fought this out in the press. How could Yoko be so blind to Paul's talent? How could Paul be so petty about the collabora-tion?

And then I realized that what interested me were the *two* narratives—the fact that two were in competition with one another.

Consider Yoko.

Narrative number one: Girlfriend arrives, gets in the way of a creative partnership and the brotherhood. Breaks up the band.

Narrative number two: Girlfriend arrives. She is herself an artist. She draws the intellectual member of the group away from the glitz, the gloss, the emptiness (and the schmaltziness) of his partner. She enables the "smart one" to grow as an artist.

Both of these narratives explain Yoko, not just her back then but her actions and statements in the years following. They also explain a lot of what Paul did post-Beatles.

Why did Yoko claim, ridiculously, that John was Mozart and Paul was the jealous Salieri? She was advocating for Narrative Number Two. Why did Paul try to change the credits on the songs? He was resisting the imposition of that narrative.

That's what I thought about when I watched the Governor's campaign. How narratives can compete. And for those living through them, a particular narrative can exert a force as powerful as gravity, so overwhelming it takes massive energy to escape from its clutches.

The Governor had three narratives to wrestle with. The first was the one Erin had said: that he was yet another politician whose greed, ego, and lust overcame him. He thought he was above the rules, he acted like a spoiled, needy child. An egomaniac. He destroyed his marriage, his family, his career, and himself.

Another narrative was one he was out there hawking. He did it all for love. That it was okay, and human, and even somewhat graceful and noble and inspiring, to be a middle-aged man and to be blindsided by love. Not sex, but love. This narrative was losing to the first.

I kept the competing narratives in mind as he entered the next phase of his campaign on the Thursday and Friday of that week. Four visits to his sons, seeking their participation, or at least their approval. Each of them refused. They all gave different reasons.

For the first three boys, the meetings ended the same way. The Governor insisted on a hug, which they permitted (awkwardly), and the Governor gave this speech:

"I respect your decision. All I ask from you is this: love your mother, love God, and find a little room in your heart to love me."

The same speech, word for word, three times. The meeting with the fourth son ended differently. He was the youngest and had been hit the hardest. He'd been forced to endure his high school's reaction to the scandal. More than that, he was the only one who still lived at home, forced to live with the toll the scandal had taken on his mother.

What led him to be the one to deliver the strongest condemnation of his father? Was he the most idealistic? The most resentful? Was it the suffering of his mother that had built up inside him?

Or was it just his personality? I found the older boys to be a little bland (not unlike their father). The youngest, John, had inherited more of his mother's fire.

"You are like a man in a Bible story," he said in the driveway of the Governor's former house. "A parable of what not to do. The man who has it all and throws it all away."

"A man," said the Governor, gentle but firm, "with love in his heart."

"It's not love, it's just selfishness," John said, spitting the words. "You're going to lose this election, and you're going to lose bad. Because nobody thinks you'd represent their interests. Everyone believes you put yourself first. And that's what they care about the most."

"I disagree. I think they care about love."

"They don't see that with you. They see sex. They see a selfish guy who ruined everything because he had to fuck some *stranger...*"

He stopped speaking. His eyes were filled with tears.

To the Governor's credit, he did not chide his son for

his language. It had to be the first time that word was ever spoken on this property. It felt like we had gone over a cliff.

The Governor stepped forward. "Son. I love you. I understand where this is coming from, I do, I do. I understand. But you'll see—this great country of ours, and this great state of ours, believe in second chances. They believe in repentance and they believe in the power of forgiveness. We'll show that. And we'll also show that the people believe in love."

It would have been nice to end there. Or with a hug. That's how I'd have directed the scene: a hug, the first one that wasn't awkward, the campaign can start, off we go. Cue the inspirational music and dissolve to a montage of baby kissing and ribbon cutting and donut eating, people laughing and waving, crowds getting bigger, maybe a scene where we stop at a gas station and kids come running from out of nowhere to high-five the Governor.

And then: the scenes with the boys. One joins, then another. John the last holdout (saved for the final third of the movie), the crowds getting bigger, the polls going up. You've seen this or a form of it a million times. Finally the holdout joins, the campaign is in full swing—and yes! Love conquers! The Governor's acceptance speech, delivered in a great hall with echoing mikes as the camera zooms in… "We have shown…that the people…believe…in love…"

Or: the Governor (and his wife! His wife and kids!) on stage, hands in the air, confetti pouring down, as the newscaster says, "They have shown…that the people…*believe*…in love…!"

Nope.

Here's what happened. The Governor stepped forward. John, who looked as if he might punch him, stepped back but not quickly enough; he pulled away as the Governor attempted a hug. The sad grapple lasted several seconds too long and required too much force. It was so painful to watch I couldn't believe I was not looking elsewhere.

John straightened up again after finally being released. Now he looked ready to run away, back to the house if the Governor attempted any more sudden movements. His eyes were still wet but he was no longer crying. Instead he looked like some kind of oracle, a young, angry prophet.

"You'll lose," he said. "You'll lose because the people believe in hate."

He stared at his father for a moment without a trace of love in his eyes. The Governor's eyes were something to behold: he was smiling, but I saw doubt and fear.

"Now son…" he said, searching for words.

John backed away a few steps. Then he turned and ran inside.

"Now son…" the Governor said quietly, still trying for words that never came and could not matter now.

In the distance the door closed.

The Governor turned to me. The mask was back on. His eyes were clear and untroubled, his smile certain.

"Ready to go?" he cried, gripping my shoulder. "We've got minds to change!"

FIVE

EARLIER I TOLD YOU THAT there were three narratives competing for the Governor's—I'm not even sure of the right word. Identity? Image? Soul? In any case, here's where we stand:

1) He was merely a politician with a "wayward pecker" (an actual quote).

2) He was a politician who followed his heart (the Governor's story).

The third was one that possibly only the Governor and I knew. It was one he'd written about over and over in his autobiography. I found it interesting—certainly deeper and more complex, on a basic human level, than anything in the other two narratives. It was also fresher. I thought it might sell books and even have some ability to enlighten an audience. I did not think it was going too far to say that this narrative could, by starting a dialogue about politicians and citizenship, generally improve the quality of our republic. Certainly it was among the top two or three most interesting ideas the Governor had.

Politicians are accused of blandness, avoiding controversy to get elected. The implication is that they know something they don't want to say, because the truth would be unpalatable to someone. So we get the handsome head saying nothing. Believe me: I'd read hundreds of pages of the Governor's innermost thoughts. There was a lot of nothing in there.

Which is why this third narrative stood out. The Governor explained that his public life made him feel false. At an event, he'd be told what to say, even given a written script by his handlers. Tina would often receive one as well. The two of them then acted out a kind of play, in which she would make a comment about him learning how to use a vacuum cleaner (this example stuck in his mind for some reason; he used it at least five times) and he would pretend to laugh and say something else scripted in return, and then go into his speech. Hugs, kisses—these were not spontaneous but carefully choreographed bits of stagecraft. During the final days of a campaign they might reenact the same skit ten times in a single day as they barnstormed across the state.

It was during his campaign for reelection that he began the affair. He could talk to his mistress. Say what he thought. *He* decided what to say. No one wrote the remarks or told him how to stand when he said them to maximize the camera angles. There was no lighting, no makeup, no audience considerations. No polls, no focus group testing. Just him, doing something he wanted. Or here's how he put it:

I didn't choose it because I wanted it. I wanted it because I had chosen it.

Fascinating! We talk a lot about the role of money in electoral politics. We complain about the idiots who run things. We blame them when they stumble. We don't think about how our expectations of them—*and their spouses*—might interfere with their ability to continue a marriage.

It's something I thought other politicians should know. If they and their spouses knew of the hazard, they could probably avoid it. I found most of the Governor's autobiography to be vapid and dull, overwhelmed by platitudes. But this at least was strange and moving:

My beloved wife Tina appeared like a robot to me at these events, as she delivered the remarks that my staff had prepared for her. I was no better. The two of us looked in each other's eyes like two machines pointed at one another. It felt alienating and subhuman, and I couldn't help thinking that it was an experience we might never recover from. Once you've seen a person in a non-genuine way...

The ellipsis destroyed me. He couldn't even *attempt* to put it in words. And yet I could fill it in.

I planned to ask the Governor about this third narrative, but the chance had not arisen. I tried at least three times; each time he cut me off with some news of the campaign. An event with fifty people. A new radio ad. Funding from out of state.

And then it hit me: *he was in a campaign now*. Had he reverted to the "dork robot in high drone mode" he described in his autobiography? Or had he put that aside this time around? His words were the same, mostly meaningless rhetoric. Did he feel true? Or false?

He had another surprise for me. He had just finished throwing out the opening pitch at a minor league baseball game ("the players don't know me but the owner's a good man," which in his code meant that the players hated him but the owner wanted some tax break or other favor). I was joining him for a drive to Muskego and a local carnival, where he planned to hang out by the midway, shaking hands.

As we got on I-43 he turned down the radio.

"Muskego's a nice place. Ever been there?"

"No."

"Good little town. After that I'm going to Italy. It's time!"

I was flabbergasted. "In the middle of the campaign?" I gasped.

"The heart has to heal."

He was waiting for a response. I couldn't say anything. Finally my silence went on so long he sensed I wasn't really buying it.

"Look: if I run as a guy who had an affair and ditched his wife, I have no chance. This isn't New York or California. Wisconsin voters are people who have learned to live within limits. Modest folks. That's who we are."

"We?" I said. I was thinking he had lived a life beyond what most people would consider modest.

"You are too," he said, misunderstanding me. "You haven't changed as much as you think."

I let this go. This wasn't about me.

"They don't want high-flyers," he went on. "You know what my aunt said to me when I told her I was running for governor? *Just don't get uppity.* Aunt Charlene, God bless her. But you know what? People here understand love. If it were just lust and sin, I'd be cooked. But falling in love, getting remarried—that's different. That's just a question of sequence. Everyone sees Ludovica as this Italian monster because she's unknown. And because they admire Tina so much. But when they get to know Ludovica, when they see the two of us together—see what we share—they'll admire her too. They'll understand why I did what I did."

He chuckled.

As we drove I assessed where he was in the race. He was still campaigning on his own. He showed up at a lot of events where there would be crowds for other reasons—the farmer's market in Madison, the art fair in New Glarus, Tommy Bartlett's water show, Summerfest. He handed out flyers he designed and printed himself. He went on radio and talk shows. But for the most part he was getting beat, and badly. The other party had put forward a solid candidate—probably the strongest female candidate Wisconsin had ever seen. She had money, and volunteers, and paid staff, and a bus. She could stage actual events that drew crowds. The Governor could not draw anyone. Coffeeshops, donut-making events, church basements. Nothing was clicking and it was getting sad. It did give him kind of an underdog status, but that was completely the opposite of what he was trying to run on.

In Menasha he spoke from the back of a fire truck, to no one. Someone gave him a bullhorn, or he took one, or something. It didn't help. An elderly woman walked past with both hands over her ears. It seemed like a metaphor for the state's response to his campaign. Italy? Why not?

I drove him to the airport.

"Long-term parking," he said, pointing at the sign.

I did as he suggested. "Why?" I asked. It was a completely innocent question—I thought maybe the security rules had changed.

"I need you to come with."

"To the airport?"

"To Italy."

I didn't know what to say. I think I may have asked why, but he said he would explain later.

"My wife—"

"She'll understand."

It had never been clearer that I had no defined role. He introduced me as his biographer. But I wasn't taking notes or planning to write about the campaign. I was just an attendee. A witness to political carnage. I suspect he liked having me there so that he did not have to be literally alone as he did this. I did not help him plan events or strategize in any way unless hearing himself talk out loud qualified as help. A lucky charm? There was no evidence that he'd had any luck at all, at least so far.

But the role he had in mind for me in Italy was even stranger:

"I need you to chaperone," he said as we were waiting to pass through security.

"Chaperone what?"

"This is a platonic visit. It has to be. I'm a married man, running for office. Can't take the risk."

I had thought the need for chaperoning was over, now that the marriage seemed to be in its final days.

"That's in the past. I need to be able to tell Tina that I was faithful."

"Why would she believe me?"

"She trusts you."

"She barely knows me."

"Why would you lie?"

He had me: I had no more loyalty to him than to her. I was surprised he'd recognized this (if that's what he'd meant).

Why did he need to be faithful now? And why did he need to go at all? He'd said something about getting engaged—or some kind of promise, since his marriage had not yet officially ended. Was this what he wanted? Or what the campaign needed? Was there a difference?

I knew if I asked this directly he'd just talk about his heart.

But I couldn't help wondering: Was he acting? Was this false? Maybe Ludovica was another character in the play?

And maybe I was, too, without knowing it. Were our conversations real? Staged? I couldn't tell what he thought. It seemed like a perpetual motion machine with only one goal, to keep moving, until the election. Would it matter if he won or lost? Would that make this seem more real? Would it be better or worse?

I kept thinking about something that had happened to me in college. I was backpacking through Europe, and I found myself alone in Madrid. It was late enough to be dark, but the streets were busy and I was making my way through the crowds, going from one set of friends to a completely different set, enjoying the night and the feeling of being young and alive and having layers of pasts that enabled me to shift from one social role to another. I turned up a side street, convinced I'd found a shortcut. It was a narrow passage, a cobblestoned street that rose up a slope, closed off to cars and with shops on both sides.

In a second I realized that something had changed. The street was filled with people, but I was the only one moving. It was as if time had literally stopped, and I was left to weave among these inert, statue-like men and women. They were handsome and beautiful and wearing nice clothes, and their faces looked made up and frozen into artificial expressions. It was like walking through a real-life wax museum, and I wondered how much goddamn sangria I'd just had to cause this hallucination. Some were in mid-stride, some were leaning on one another, as if in conversation. The light was weird. I walked through as best I could, feeling like I was floating. I wanted to poke someone but didn't dare. I was the only one alive, but oddly my first thought was that I had died. Was this what happened? Maybe the world freezes in place and you just wander around. Because what else could it be? A wormhole? Some kind of twilight zone?

When I reached the top of the street I realized that a man with a megaphone, sitting in the bucket of a crane, was directing a movie, and I had just wandered onto the set. In fact, he was yelling one thing, over and over, which was to tell me to get the fuck off his set. I spoke no Spanish but didn't need to. The fury behind his words was universal.

And now, there I was: on a plane, flying to Italy. It felt just like that night in Madrid. Everyone else belonged here but I didn't, only this time the people were real and it was I who wasn't.

The Governor ate two bags of peanuts, put on a blindfold, and didn't wake up until our wheels skidded along the runway.

LUDOVICA LAMBERTUCCI, AS I AND EVERYONE who had followed the Governor knew, was an Italian television journalist who had met the Governor a year into his second term. She'd been doing a profile on governors who had turned down federal money out of principle. I still resented this decision of his, incidentally, as it would have put high-speed rail from Chicago to Minneapolis via Madison, which would have been a significant positive development for those of us who believe that travel is a good thing and that Wisconsinites could use a little more Minneapolis and a lot more Chicago in their lives. The Governor said I wasn't qualified to express an opinion because I had moved away. Maybe he was right, who knows.

In any case, Ludovica, or "La Ludo" as she was known throughout Italy, was elegant and dynamic and smoldering, "Sophia Loren to Tina's Grace Kelly," as the Governor put it in his memoirs. Which does one prefer? La Ludo had olive skin and reddish-brown hair she wore either wild and sprawling or pulled tight and smooth. She favored big bracelets and carried big purses and had big shoulders.

Footage has emerged of the two of them bantering, flirting, which was taken during the filming of the documentary but did not make it into the finished product. The Governor is so awkward it's painful to watch. He's like a man who's never so much as flirted before now trying to get laid, a fifteen-year-old trying to seduce a woman in her forties. They also exchanged emails—which were made public later, somehow or other—that show him in a more flattering light. I knew the timeline from the biography: after the taped segments and the emails, they'd met for a few off-camera interviews, then another after the report had aired. She seemed thrilled to have this highly placed source, who in turn seemed just as bedazzled. True love? I guess.

They soon fell into a more physical affair, meeting secretly in hotels in Chicago, New York, and Rome.

Based on news headlines I'd had the impression that a kind of chill had set in between them. The Governor assured me I'd been mistaken.

"She can't wait to see me," he said as we stood waiting to get our bags out of the overhead bins.

I nodded without much enthusiasm. I was groggy from the flight, but also—why should I care? Why should I be excited? I wanted a cappuccino or a bed. This was not my lover we were talking about.

"She's meeting us at baggage," the Governor said. "Is that romantic or what?"

I felt like I was in his way. "I'm the chaperone, right? I can leave you alone if you want."

I'd be happy to do that. Very, very happy.

"Don't worry, it won't be that hard," he said. "I'll be good. I won't try to trick you or anything." He sighed. "Those days are behind me."

He closed his eyes for a moment. He was sucking a breath mint. Then he opened them again as the line started to move. He clapped my shoulder.

"Are you ready for this?"

Something shifted in me and I started to feel the excitement. It was morning outside; the air felt different, here in Rome, even though we were still on the plane.

"It doesn't feel real," I said.

"Oh it's real." The line paused. The Governor tapped me on the shoulder until I turned around. He pulled a small box from his shoulder bag and snapped it open. A gold ring, with a diamond.

"As real as this," he said with a goofy grin.

The line was moving again.

In the airport he sort of forgot about me, moving quickly, stopping in the bathroom, zigzagging around, eyes always trying to see ahead, beyond the crowds. Twice he went the wrong way, and I followed stupidly, trying to point out the sign he'd missed, until he realized his mistake as if I had not said anything. I offered to wait for the bags and catch up to him on the other side of the passport check, but he ignored me. I got the sense he needed to wait for the bags too: his nervous energy was brimming over, and he didn't want to go too long without doing something useful.

After our bags came we got in a very long line for customs. We were still at the airport but I felt the pull of Rome nevertheless. Those glorious faces, with their ancient heritage (probably imagined on my part but amazing nonetheless), restaurants serving up peas and fava beans and globe artichokes and lamb's milk cheese, the Vespas whizzing along the ancient stone streets. By the time we emerged, dazed, into the main terminal, I could not wait to see the city again. Bernini fountains! SPQR on the manhole covers!

"Mr. Olson?"

It was a man with dark curly hair that didn't cover all of his head. Sort of a comb-over for curly hair, is the only way I can describe it.

"I am the brother," he said. "The brother of The Ludo."

His English was passable with a smile-inducing accent. Who was I to judge? My Italian was limited.

The Governor, I soon realized, had less than none. "Ciao, amigo!" he said, pumping the man's hand, then throwing an arm around him as if the man were one of the Governor's supporters.

The man cringed and half ducked. He did not look happy. "La Ludo, she cannot make it here today," he said.

"Of course!" the Governor said, though it was clear he was disappointed. "She sent you to retrieve us. Lead on, *maestro!*"

This last word had the worst rolled R I have ever heard in my life. It was at least four syllables and included a D sound and, if I'm not mistaken, an aspirated B.

The brother nodded, not quite understanding. "Yes. You need to go home."

"Home with you? Or—well, where is La Ludo? At work? We'll go there."

"No. Home in the U.S.A. *America*," he clarified.

The Governor glanced at me and smiled at the man. "We may be having a *problem in translation*," he said, as if he were an ESL teacher introducing a cliché to a classroom of students. "But my friend, your English is twice as good as my *Italiano*."

It was like campaign mode: he was acting. Did he have any other way of interacting with someone he'd just met?

I noticed a pair of police officers watching us. They didn't seem to like the fact that we were just standing there. One pointed at us. The other nodded slowly. They were both holding automatic weapons.

"She does not want to see you," said the man. "*Does not want*. I will help you to buy the new ticket." He waved an arm behind him, I guess to point out another part of the airport, the place where they sold tickets. He smiled at me: he'd buy me one too. I smiled back. This was all so absurd.

"Oh, we don't need help with that, sir," said the Governor, suddenly formal. "We're here to see Ludovica Lambertucci."

Some general confusion followed. The man tried to get our attention and spoke some more in Italian, but the Governor pushed past him, holding nothing, as if we would head out to Rome by ourselves, without even our bags. The man watched us leave and finally turned in another direction. But then, after we were halfway to the taxi stand, the Governor suddenly turned and started to follow the man down the corridor.

We were faster than he was and caught up to him at the sliding doors that went to the *parcheggio*.

Here he noticed us.

"Do not follow me!" he shouted. Except that he was outside the sliding doors and we were inside; the doors slid shut halfway through his sentence.

"Do not!"—the doors closed—"Follow me!" he shouted through the glass. They slid open again. "Do not—" The doors slid shut again. "Follow me!" he shouted again, louder this time, more frustrated.

He turned and hurried away. We followed him out the doors.

"It's okay, *amigo*," said the Governor when we caught up. "We just want to go with you. To get in your car," he added, as if that were ever "okay" to someone who has told you several times not to follow him. Our bags were somewhere behind us.

The man, who was a full head shorter than the Governor and me, began to racewalk down the aisles of the *parcheggio*, cutting between cars, trying to ditch us.

"Sir! Sir! Man! Amigo!" the Governor shouted as we walked, then jogged after him.

The man stopped and shouted something angry in Italian, then turned and went into a full sprint. We ran after him. His green jacket was riding up on his back; I could see the striped shirt underneath. I was not at all sure what we were doing.

We passed a long black Mercedes and a door suddenly opened. A woman got out and called after the man, who circled back.

"Ludo!" the Governor cried, coming to a halt. He walked toward her, his arms out. "Darling!" he cried.

She was wearing sunglasses and looked more fashionable than anyone I had ever seen. She looked like a movie star. She was wearing a cream-colored suit and had dark eyebrows that curved nicely but did not move, and beautiful full lips. Her hair looked fantastic, flowing away from her head as if she'd been on a motorcycle, but every strand had somehow remained in place. She did look older than I'd expected but she did not look as old as she was.

The Governor went in to kiss her on the cheek, the casual Italian way, a minimal greeting. Not an offensive one under ordinary circumstances. She held up her hand. "No," she said, in such a commanding voice I wanted to turn around and head back to the States. It was a voice that spoke for all of Italy. Thousands of years of civilization were behind it.

"No why?" said the Governor.

"I told you not to come here."

The Governor chuckled, awkwardly pretending she had not just blocked his attempt to kiss her. He was breathing hard from our run.

"I wrote it in an email," she said. "Wrote it in very clear words."

"I could tell what was between the lines."

"You need to leave. This is not acceptable."

"Well, now…" said the Governor, as the man we'd been chasing rejoined us. He looked like he might collapse. "Things have changed."

"You're running for another office."

"U.S. Congress."

"You are losing. I've studied the polls. Your *numbers*. You have *no* chance."

Her voice was beautiful. It was no wonder he'd been attracted to her. What seemed surprising was that she had ever been attracted to him.

"Let's take a step back," he said. "That's not the change I meant…"

"It's a bad idea to run," she said. "America will not accept it. *Puritanismo*."

I thought I had some insight into their relationship, just from that single word and the way in which she said it. She didn't love him, and maybe she never had. She loved America, loved being an Italian with a serious knowledge of America. She didn't need the Governor. She could find another American with whom to explore her theories.

The Governor did not see it this way, of course. "We

can do this," he said. "You'll see—the people are ready. For you. For us. Come on the trail with me. You can bring cameras, bring the crew. Who was that guy, Giobanni?"

"Giovanni."

"Bring Giobanni, it'll be great to see him again. It'll be the comeback story of the century, and you'll be there for it. You're a journalist, and we're in love, and it makes perfect sense—they'll probably make a movie out of this someday. Cinema."

She stared at him until he finished speaking. "You're a joke now," she said. (In her accent this came out as "choke.")

"What we have is *special*," he said. He put his hand in the front pocket of his shoulder bag. *Don't do it,* I thought. *Do not pull out the ring.* At the same time I wanted to see it happen.

"It's not special," said La Ludo. "It is a *nothing*. We have a *nothing*. I do not love you. I do not have the respect for you. I do not want to see you. Anymore! Ever again!"

He smiled. "I know you don't mean that. Here, dear," he said, pulling out the box.

It had to be the worst proposal in the history of marriage. Here, dear? It was as though the English language had been held up at customs.

He opened the box. She gasped and batted it out of his hand. Then she and the man got in the car, one of them shouting, the other shrieking. Both doors slammed. I thought they might run us over.

Finally her window began to roll down and her door opened, as if she could not even wait for the window, or as if she were too angry to think clearly. "I hate you," she said. "Leave this country. And so you know, you will lose!"

Then she looked around the parking lot as if to make sure no one had witnessed any of this—she was of course a famous person in Italy, and a cell phone video could have been disastrous. Her door slammed shut, the window rolled up, and they drove away.

I was already up on the sidewalk, away from danger, but the Governor had to step back to avoid their crazy swerve as they backed out and took off down the aisle.

There was no grace at all to his movements; the humiliation was complete. He looked stunned and I felt terrible for him. What narrative would this be? How could he turn this around? There was no positive spin that I could see. He probably wished—and I wished on his behalf—that there had not even been one witness. I wished that for my sake as well as his. Some things you can't unsee. It would help him to pretend that this whole incident had not happened, which was the only way forward that I could imagine.

I picked up the box and handed it to him, but the ring had rolled under a Punto. I kneeled down to try to retrieve it. It seemed like the least I could do.

"Leave it," he said. "That's for La Ludo. It's no good to me now."

"If she changes her mind…?" I actually managed not to laugh as I said this.

"Then I'll get her another one. A *new* one!"

It was so pathetic, the way he said *new*, but already I could hear him start to recover his optimism. I should have known it would happen.

We walked back into the airport. Our bags had been confiscated. They sat in a room tended by a lonely little man. He had put them on two different shelves, as if they had been bad and could not enjoy one another's company.

We went back to the ticket counter in silence. It suddenly felt like I had been awake forever.

"I wonder who that guy was," the Governor said.

"He said he was her brother."

"She doesn't have a brother."

He did not seem tired and I thought he might talk about adversity, comebacks, and the healing heart. Not this time. We sat in silence until it was time to board our flight back to Chicago. We were not seated next to one another, which I chose to view as a sign of my own.

I slept most of the way. When I woke up, the woman next to me was drinking red wine. "They brought me the whole bottle," she said. "I had them bring an extra glass in case you woke up."

"*Viva Italia*," I said as she filled my plastic cup.

Later I made my way down the aisle and walked past the Governor, who had the row to himself. He was wearing his sleep mask and he was not smiling, though he was clearly not asleep, either.

"What? Did you say something?" he asked. There was nobody there. Nobody had said anything. I didn't want to answer because he'd recognize my voice, and I had nothing to say. But for some reason I couldn't leave.

"Who? What?" he said.

He "looked" around, back and forth, dumbly unaware. At first I thought he looked like a stupid, damaged insect, a comic image if somewhat cruel. But then I thought of a prisoner blindfolded in the dark, unsure if he was having a nightmarish hallucination or if he'd just heard the clicking sounds of the firing squad cocking their rifles.

I stood there for another second or two, marveling at the sight, before I finally crept away.

SIX

B Y SEPTEMBER EVERYONE WAS TIRED of the Governor. The voters were, anyway. The pundits were just getting started.

For me it was surreal: I would attend a campaign event that had ten people in the room, if one generously counted a couple of venue staff. The Governor would do three or four of those a day, in Elkhorn and Beloit and Mt. Pleasant and Caledonia. A local reporter might show up toward the end and ask a few questions. Sometimes a blogger.

What were these like? He held one such event in Madison, on State Street—returning students streaming past, the Governor shouting to be heard above a street philosopher (who'd drawn a larger crowd). We'd hang around a sports bar in Kenosha during a Packers game—I and everyone else would watch the game while the Governor tried to make himself relevant. We went to Miller Park before a Brewers game and were chased away by a couple of vigilant security guards.

The Governor's enthusiasm was higher than ever. "They love me in Whitewater!" he would cry as we drove to yet another church breakfast. Nobody was there for him. They didn't love him in Whitewater. They didn't love him anywhere. They were tepid at best. I began to wonder if that was his goal: if he *aspired* to indifference.

What made this surreal, other than the Governor's enthusiasm in the face of total indifference, was that after one of these events, after the craziest bottoming out (*two people* at a lutefisk dinner in Union Grove, or maybe it was being drowned out by "pop music superstars" Air Supply—*Air Supply*—at the Walworth County Fair), I would get back to the hotel and turn on the television and see the media's fixation on the Governor. Nationally he was bigger than ever. There were late-night jokes, of course (he was the "philanderer who sneaks around trying to fool his wife" du jour). But he had also regained some of the mojo with a certain kind of pundit who has overcome his or her natural inability to say anything interesting or accurate, or to have any personally appealing qualities, by instinctively taking the contrarian's view of any issue. That was his fan base. And they hated him too.

During one of my two-day stints in D.C. my wife and I spent an evening in the basement watching these luminaries. Some idiot on a cable channel was saying he thought the race was the Governor's to lose.

"Is that *true*?" my wife asked me.

"It's not what I'm seeing on the ground," I told her.

"There's a *groundswell!*" the pundit said at that moment.

You can always claim there's a silent majority on your side. They are silent, after all. Silent people will not contradict you until the election. Maybe that's why idiots like them so much.

Other pundits took a more thoughtful view. The Governor was losing, they acknowledged, but he was bringing good issues into the campaign, which was itself a victory and probably all he hoped for.

"Is that why he's running?" my wife asked. "To get issues into the campaign?"

"He never talks about issues," I told her.

"This is a man who cares about issues!" the television

man shouted at me.

Others were sympathetic: they liked him, they wished him well, and isn't it a shame that America is hung up on bedroom scandals. In France they think we're crazy.

"He has the cheater vote locked up," my wife observed.

It gave the Governor some hope—more people knew his name than his opponent's—but it was hard for me to see how this free negative publicity was going to help. When a late night comedian asks the audience if they know the difference between Governor Olson and Adolph Hitler, does the punch line matter? (Hitler's staff always knew where he was. Is that funny? I didn't think so. It got a big laugh, or at least it did after the host made a kind of grimace. It shows you how easy it was to punch the Governor Olson button in those weeks.)

My friends Ross and Erin were fascinated by the Americanness of the campaign. They'd never followed one closely before.

"He's doomed!" Ross said. "Why's he doing this? He has no chance!"

I told them the story of a trip we made to Kenosha and the two college kids who came up to him after he'd delivered a speech. They were not supporters. I thought it was obvious but they fooled the Governor.

"Can I have your autograph?" one asked.

"Of course."

She pulled her shirt down, exposing the top half of her breast. The other woman handed the Governor a pen.

"Sign her boob," she said.

The Governor frowned and shook his head.

"It's okay—she's Italian!" the woman said.

The Governor looked like a parent about to give a lecture. "Young lady, I will not," he said.

The women cackled and scampered away.

The Governor had been through a lot, and he faced most of it with a smile, but this made him distraught.

"And you really want to represent these people?" I said, trying to kid him out of his funk.

It worked, in a way. "Yes. They need guidance!" he snapped.

Usually I'm opposed to this sort of attitude, but I couldn't really disagree with him. "I guess they do," I mumbled.

"We *all* do," he said magnanimously.

Ross and Erin nodded, trying to understand. I had not understood any of this exchange myself, really. It was an example of how strange it all was. They needed guidance, the Governor needed guidance...but everyone else? Me? Governor Snowmobile was going to guide us? He would channel God and deliver sermons?

"And then you came home and started reading books about Cato," my wife said.

"I had an idea I wanted to explore."

"You care more about the past than the present."

"I think I care too much about the present," I said. "The present hurts too much."

"He's doomed, isn't he?" Ross asked.

Doomed might have been a little strong. There were still a few ways for him to turn this around. There were debates scheduled for October. There was the possibility that Tina would involve herself somehow: she remained massively popular, and if she decided to join the Governor on the trail (as he hoped), there might be time for a surge. I supposed his opponent could die again, horrible as that sounded. It was at least theoretically possible. None of these scenarios seemed likely. Tina still hated him. And his opponent was young, healthy, and a good public speaker. She appeared likely both to trounce him in the debates and stay alive.

Paige Perkins was a popular UW alum who'd been a software developer, then vice president, and finally CEO of a respectable company that was based in Wisconsin and now employed over a thousand people. She was the face of good jobs, decent wages, health benefits, and staying local. Her business had solar panels on the roof and Odwalla bars in the break room. She also had a brother who'd tragically lost his legs in Afghanistan; he lived with her and her husband. One of her main causes had been to get him and other veterans the help they needed, and her company had patented a new form of artificial knee that had apparently revolutionized the prosthetic limb industry.

How could the Governor compete? She was a candidate dreamed up by the DNC, complete with a few independent streaks (she was in favor of charter schools and capital punishment). She was well known, smart, popular, and likable. She ran a clean and efficient campaign. Even her inexperience worked in her favor: she represented a fresh start (the Governor did not seem old in life but by comparison he seemed like he'd been around forever). And it helped that she was pretty in a Wisconsin kind of way. She had reigned as the Dairy Princess of Walworth County not that long before.

I was with the Governor, in a green room, while a cable channel ran a clip. The Governor's second-oldest son had a Paige Perkins bumper sticker ("Time To Turn The Paige!") on his car.

I forced myself to glance at the Governor, whose face was contorted in the long-form version of a wince.

"I can't believe they run that garbage as *news*," he said. "What happened to standards?"

I pushed back without thinking. "Betrayal is always news."

He regarded me with astonishment. "That's my *son*."

I didn't know how to respond.

"One of my enemies must have put it there."

I asked him who his enemies were. I meant it seriously. I was genuinely interested: it seemed more compelling in this environment of constant, unrelenting indifference. Enemies suggested a kind of relevance that was not otherwise in evidence.

He smiled. "I take the point," he said. "It's a political term, one we use in politics. What I have is more accurately described as a lot of undecideds. But you're right: I have no enemies, and for that I should be grateful."

That hadn't been my point at all, neither the underlying fact nor the lesson learned, but there was no time to discuss this further (if you count our skew-line monologues to be a discussion), because at that moment an assistant producer escorted us to the studio and the Governor was soon sitting in front of a green screen (which became the Capitol building on air) for a remote with a wonky political show jointly hosted by a man and woman in New York and D.C.

"Governor, thank you for joining us on *The Chatter*."

"My pleasure…Chad."

The Governor adjusted his earpiece and the cord draped across the back of his head. The contorted position of his arm made him look like an ape scratching himself, which was not really his fault, but the hole in the underarm of his jacket was his fault. And the pause before the name: he got the right name, at least, but he looked lost in trying to recover it.

He was off and running.

"Governor," Chad began. "Let's look at some polls." He explained the numbers on the screen. "In Wisconsin your party is slightly behind. Fifty-one forty-nine. Within the margin of error."

The Governor nodded.

"In your district, your hometown, your party runs ahead. Fifty-eight forty-two. And here are your numbers…"

Some information came on the screen, with a small photo of the Governor smiling, which made him look clueless in the face of the atrocious news.

"You're down seventy-four twenty-five in the state."

"Well, I think you said it best," said the Governor. "There is a margin of error."

"Not this big…And here are the numbers for your district. Governor, this includes your friends, your neighbors, your family…the people you grew up with. And you are down seventy-nine to twenty. A *fifty-nine* point deficit. Governor, the people who know you best seem to like you the least."

"Chad, I can't worry about polls. I'm just trying to get my message out."

"Fair point, Governor," said Chad. "What's your message? The role of government in our lives?"

"The role of love in our hearts."

Chad and Valerie, his New York-based counterpart, paused, each waiting for the other to speak. Finally Chad took off his glasses and held them before his chin—his Serious Journalist look. "Governor, with respect. Are you the best person to base a campaign on a message of love?"

The Governor smiled, a dopey rabbit hopping into the trap.

"Absolutely I am."

"Because your wife was asked this question just yesterday. Here's what she said."

A set of quotes came on the screen. Chad read them in his newsman voice.

"Quote. 'The Governor doesn't know what marriage is. He doesn't know what loyalty and honesty are. And he has no clue what love is.' Care to respond?"

"She may have been misquoted."

"It's *The New York Times*, sir. They've posted the entire transcript on their website."

"It doesn't matter. Look. I hurt her. She has every right to lash out. I deserve it, Chad."

"And?"

"And that's it."

"But you're still the person to carry this message?"

"Absolutely."

"Because you've repented?"

"Because I've *suffered*." He was sincere when he said

this—it came through in his tone and his face. Even Valerie picked up on it:

"You're still suffering, aren't you, Governor?"

"Absolutely I am." Now he was wearing his mask again. "But I'm looking forward."

"Are you looking forward to the debates?"

"Of course."

"And I—we heard this morning that your wife has scheduled a press conference."

I was sure the Governor hadn't heard about this, because otherwise it would have been the only thing he'd have talked about.

"Good for her," he said, without a flinch.

"Are you looking forward to that too?"

There was a long pause—thirty-five seconds, as the whole Internet would soon know, as the video went viral and it became a kind of contest to fill the gap with something meaningful—the Gettysburg address, movie dialogue, the audio of Homer Simpson falling off a cliff.

You literally could see the Governor turn colors as the blood rushed away from his face. Finally he smiled. "Valerie, I look forward to life."

It was a total meltdown: the strange, glassy look in his eyes, the stiff delivery.

My wife called during a commercial break. "This is bigger than the snowmobiling thing!" she said. "It's breaking the Internet." She was watching it as we spoke. "He doesn't look *human*."

It seemed like a good time to test the theory on my wife. I was still in charge of the book, and my wife would be the type of person we'd need to reach if we were going to break out of the minimal sales of the 500 or so in the chattering classes, who probably didn't even buy books anyway, basing their opinion on a website's version of it. Without customers like my wife, generally intelligent people with a mild interest in politics but not an obsession, we might sell one copy.

"He wrote about how this happens to candidates. And those close to them. They become like actors in a play."

"He needs better lines."

After the break they had an interview with Paige Perkins, who was standing in front of a photo of a red barn on a hill.

"What can I say?" she was saying. "I think we all hope he's doing well."

"Do you—watching the interview we just did—do you think he's *not* well?"

"I think he's gone through a lot," she said, careful not to offend but basically destroying him. "I'm not a doctor or a clinical psychiatrist. But I think his personal issues make it difficult for him to lead. I wish him the best, health-wise."

Valerie did not want to let this drop; it was news. "Do you think he should drop out? Maybe get some help?"

"That's not for me to say."

In the aftermath of all this a new poll came out. The Governor's numbers had dropped another four points. He was entering Dick Cheney territory. A new question was included in one of them:

"Do you believe Governor Olson is stable?"

Eighty-six percent said no.

"Well, who is stable," said the Governor when I asked him about this. "Life's not stable. Right?"

I said something feeble about it being a vague question to ask people on the phone, and that there were probably nuances not captured in the binary yes-or-no suggested response.

"This is poised to be the greatest comeback in history!" he cried. "This book will have a crackerjack ending!"

I smiled faintly, and then a strange thing happened. I tried to muster up some enthusiasm to match his, but the effort was so at odds with what I really felt that it withered and died in the span of about two seconds. Halfway through my response, as I repeated the word *crackerjack*—I was in disbelief at the word *and* the concept—my voice suddenly abandoned me altogether, like a car engine giving up in the extreme cold. This happened halfway through the word, so I kicked up some phony enthusiasm—I stepped on the accelerator—but this was way too hard, so I wound up making the second half of the word much too energetic.

GOVERNOR: This book will have a crackerjack ending!

ME: Cracker…JACK!

It was false and horrible. This work, being around him, was making me miserable. But the Governor just grinned and clapped his hands together, just one clap, which he then held, as I backed away, ashamed of my duplicity.

SEVEN

WHEN I WAS YOUNG, MY CLASS took a field trip to the Museum of Science and Industry. On the way back from Chicago we stopped at a McDonald's, and along with the meal everyone received a Monopoly game piece. It was a small square piece of cardboard with the monocle man—Uncle Pennybags—on the front and two perforated tabs running down each side. On the back were rules and the red text in the Monopoly font. And the magic words:

WIN $1,000,000

Everyone else tore theirs open. A couple of kids won—a small fries, an apple pie. I put mine in my pocket and got busy with other things. I had a meal to eat, friends to hang out with—I don't know why I didn't open mine. I just didn't.

I was astonished by the reaction. On the bus, everyone went crazy with the rumor—I hadn't opened mine yet! What was in there? What was I waiting for?

For some reason this made me decide not to open it. I didn't want to be on display. I figured I'd open it later. So I refused.

By the time we returned to the school parking lot I was surrounded by other kids.

"When you gonna open it?"

"Yeah, when? Come on."

"I might not," I said. "I might never open it."

"Come *on*. S'amillion dollars."

They could not fathom my refusal. People got angry. They did not forget about it. I waited. Days went by, then a week, then another, until I began to realize that it meant more unopened than opened. It was a one in 80 million chance of winning the big prize—infinitesimal odds I could live with defying—and who cared about the smaller prizes? Not opening it was worth more than a small Coke.

I kept it in my wallet. I never brought it up. Once in a while a rumor would spread that I'd opened it, and I would produce the piece to verify that I hadn't.

I became a freak: the kid who turned down a million dollars. The rumor spread to other schools. At parties I'd be pointed at—yeah, *that's* the guy. The guy with the Monopoly thing. Never opened it. He'll show it to us if we bug him about it.

The toughest kid in school grabbed me one day and shoved me against a locker.

"Dude. I admire your willpower."

"Thank you."

"No I don't, you idiot. You're so stupid. You could be a millionaire right now and not even know it."

I saw fury in his eyes and felt lucky when he decided to leave me alone.

I got wind of a plot: a group of seniors planned to demand inspection, then attack me, hold me down, pull my shirt over my head (why this was necessary I didn't know, but it was an essential step), grab the piece out of my hand, and rip it open, exposing its contents to the world, once and for all. I thwarted this by leaking some counterintelligence. Soon the news spread: the piece was secured in my father's safety deposit box at the impregnable Farmers & Merchants Bank. It was a fiction: the thing remained in my wallet the entire time. Once in a while I would show it to someone, though I was careful about how and when, demanding a five-foot buffer between me and the lucky onlookers.

I was starting to believe in the power of this thing, not as a talisman but as a phenomenon. It had to mean something that it—and I—had generated so much consternation. I represented something. To some I was a testament to discipline, to conviction, to inner strength. To others I was a fool who needed to be saved. To many I was both. And to a few I became a symbol of something horrible, something wrong with the world, or humanity; I needed to be exposed as a fraud. Whatever I represented, the principle on which I stood, needed to be expunged.

I started receiving threats. Violence seemed real. Would I die for this?

I stopped showing the thing to people altogether. This forced them to accept my word for it that it still existed. For all they knew, I had opened it long ago. The only thing they had to go on was what I told them was the truth.

The school divided into two groups. Believers and doubters.

The contest ended, and I would no longer be able to redeem the prize. It didn't matter. People were just as agitated—now it was the fact that I didn't know and didn't want to know. They could not believe I wouldn't open it now—before, I guess, they thought I didn't want my life to change. Now I didn't possess the requisite amount of curiosity. Except for those who didn't believe me: who thought I had opened it, learned I didn't win, and then pretended otherwise. A small sect claimed I had won the million dollars but had not informed anyone for fear of exposing myself to attacks.

I didn't view this as anything other than a kind of anthropological experiment. I was alone in a sea of insanity. I began to wonder if maybe I should lock the thing up as I had said. I didn't know where this was headed or what I was supposed to do, but it felt like I should exercise some control, take some precautionary measures. Take my responsibility to this phenomenon seriously. It was getting beyond me.

OUR HUMAN ANATOMY TEACHER, Ted Knipschild, was a friendly guy, very funny, and although he was a minister on the weekends he was not above making the occasional mildly dirty joke. Not anything mean-spirited or crass, just a double entendre, a winking reference to sex—edgy for my high school, where the teachers tended toward the parochial and reserved. He was popular, even beloved, and he performed many weddings for recent graduates.

I was not totally on board. I liked his personality, but I found the God side of him to be a little pious. Even then I had trouble with religion and the demands it made on me. I could not get out of my mind the smugness with which religion fought its way out of logical blind alleys with non-answers like "mysterious ways" or "not our place to question Him."

One day in class Mr. Knipschild finished early. He sat down on his desk, his favorite place to give us a little life lesson. He swung his legs and pushed his glasses higher on his nose, and told us all that he'd been thinking a lot about me, and about the Monopoly game piece that I'd kept in my wallet for the past few months. He walked the class through the story of what had happened and what he thought it meant. It was like a sermon, and it probably was—he had probably drafted it for his Sunday congregation and was using our class as a dry run. It would not have been the first time.

Sitting there, listening, I was not comfortable. I didn't

think it was appropriate. In fact I'd objected before when he'd injected religion into our class. I had pointed out logical flaws and later told him that there were Constitutional prohibitions against what he was doing. Now he told the class that I had taught them all a lesson about the power of faith, that I had shown them the power of mystery, and that this was true in a broader sense of life as well.

I was offended that he would use me in this way.

Suddenly I believed I had my mission: this was the moment it had all been building to. I knew what needed to be done. I would walk to the front of the room, face him, pull out my wallet—oh, this would be perfect! I could show everyone the piece, the great source of belief and the power of mystery and miracle, and rip off the edges. Then I would announce what was there: One Quarter Pounder with Cheese! Or one McChicken Sandwich! Or best of all: Try again next time!

It flashed into my mind that the worst-case scenario would be if the piece were a winner: what if it was a million dollars? And I had turned it down! I would look like a total fool.

This actually crossed my mind—I had never before thought that it actually might be a winner. But now, with complete humiliation on the line, I thought it was not only possible but likely: if I chose that moment to open it, the ticket would be a winner. I don't know where this view came from but it seemed to me to be a virtual certainty.

But no! In the end I sat still, made no face, did not sigh or roll my eyes. I let him deliver his sermon—who cared? Whatever I was doing with this thing was bigger than that. It was not worth sacrificing it for him or for anyone else. I had turned into a believer in some sense. I believed in it, though I would have struggled to explain what *it* was.

I know what he would have said: this was *belief*, and once you know you can possess *belief*, even in the face of *rationality*, then you are on God's turf. If you are not yet knocking at his door, you have anyway started on the path that will lead you there.

His words streamed past me like wind in a tunnel, but my expression did not change. I sat there with my principles, saying nothing, wishing I had a better sense of what I should do, and why.

Why did I matter? I wished I knew.

THE CAMPAIGN LURCHED INTO OCTOBER. Both sides claimed they would debate as often as possible, anytime, anywhere, because it was important to get the issues out there. Et cetera. After this commitment to democracy they started setting conditions. Certain dates were ruled out, and venues, and moderators, until in the end the anytime, anywhere, as often as possible had turned into a single 75-minute debate, with pre-vetted questions. I'm told that this is more or less how these things typically turn out. The moderators were a mix of local news (print and television) and a host from a national news radio program.

The venue was an auditorium at UW-Parkside. I attended in person. I was not in the wings for this one, but in the audience like any other citizen. From this vantage point the empty stage looked like a dock on a pond nobody visited.

Ten minutes before the debate began, the Governor and his opponent took the stage. The Governor peered out at the audience, shielding his eyes with his hand, looking for someone. Finally he waved, and I turned in my seat. This was news—had one of his sons shown up? Some other supporter? But who?

I turned back and realized he was waving at *me*.

It's not fun to feel pity for someone in his fifties, who's not sick or starving, but whose life has crumbled around him. It was his fault, sure—I'm not denying that—but I couldn't avoid the pity in my stomach as I smiled feebly and waved back. And like all pity, this was laced with contempt that I tried to resist. Contempt why? For having only me.

But he waved again, and pointed and smiled, until I realized that he had no choice. He had to do something. Political survival demanded it. His opponent was surrounded by loved ones, kids, nieces, nephews, her husband, her loving in-laws. Her adorable two-year-old son rushed the stage, his hair combed, a blue-and-yellow tie around his neck. She hugged him, scooped him up onto the crook of her arm—*and took a packet of crackers out of her pocket and gave it to him*—and this was on camera! This was her first time running for office, but already she was masterful. (The video went viral; you can still see it with a little searching.) And it seemed to me that she did not yet possess the degree of cynicism that would have made it tough to pull this off without looking like a fraud. She had faced no real criticism. Had not been forced to make an unpopular choice. Had alienated no one. Her fundraising had been simple and pure.

Give her a few years in D.C. and that laugh would sound hollow. That fresh smile of hers would look like a mask.

But now it was not, now it was sweet, a tableau that makes you proud of America. I actually choked up—I, the Governor's only supporter (who could not even vote in this state)—was overcome by motherhood and family. The tear in my eye told me the race was over. The Governor had no chance.

But he was a professional. He started well. In his opening he framed his apology smoothly. He limited his references to his heart, then said he wanted now to focus on the issues. He made a credible assertion that he believed in doing the job that the people would elect him to do. He knew it would involve hard work; he was ready. He'd done it before and would do it again, if given the chance.

His opponent listened to all of this with a stern expression on her face. When he smiled and asked for forgiveness, her face grew tighter. When it was over, she looked at the moderator, waiting for the signal that it was her time to speak. Then she unloaded the following:

"Yes, I agree that the people of Wisconsin need someone who will focus on the issues. You all know his positions; you're learning what mine are. I trust that he has some good ideas; I think I have better ones. You can read them and think it through for yourselves.

"But tonight I want to talk about character. I want to talk about what this man did to his wife, and his children, and the people of this state. It is inexcusable. There simply is no other word.

"I happen to love Tina Olson. I think she is an amazing person and I was proud to have her as our state's First Lady. And to see what he did to her"—here she turned to the Governor—"to think about what *you* did to her, takes me to a place I do not want to be. I think it happened to a lot of us. We *hated* you.

"I know it's easy to say we love the sinner and hate the sin—we all try to do that, and sometimes—often—it's appropriate.

"And sometimes, Governor, it is not. You have not shown forgiveness. You talk about your heart as if it's the only thing in the world that matters. I've seen you on the campaign trail, I've heard you for months, and I say this: the people are not ready to trust you, Governor, and they shouldn't be. You haven't earned that.

"Governor Olson, we loved your wife and loved your kids. We still do. And we hated what you did to them. We hated *you*.

"I know people are trying to get beyond that. Some may have forgiven you. I haven't. *I hate you.* I want to tell everyone that it's okay to live with that feeling too. It can be okay, sometimes, to hate."

She was charming and compelling, with her dairy princess smile and her fresh, dewy eyes. The audience applauded—they actually applauded this, this ode to hate, I guess because they felt relieved to hear her say aloud what they themselves had felt. But I still thought she had taken this too far. She had left an opening for the Governor, an experienced and at times masterful politician, to turn this into a battle of negativity against forgiveness. She had had the better angels argument; now, with one speech, offering hate as a platform, she had left that to him.

Instead the Governor waited for the applause to die down. Then he looked at the moderator.

"I think she went over her time," he said.

The moderator laughed. "No journalist in the *world* would have stopped *that*."

The Governor smiled, still looking pained. "Well, let's keep things fair," he said. "I'd appreciate it."

The moderator could barely suppress her smile. "Of course. Do you want to respond to that, Governor, or go to the first question?"

"I'd like to respond," he said.

This was followed by eighteen awful seconds of silence.

"Governor?" said the moderator. "Respond?"

"I meant respond to the first question," he said, with the same frozen smile. "I'm waiting for you to ask me about something else."

It was a terrible bit of stagecraft: the writers of *Saturday Night Live* could take the week off.

The debate continued but never really got beyond that moment. Everyone knew it was over—the whole campaign ended, I would say, in those eighteen seconds.

And the book? How would this end the book? The Governor would maybe allow a sentence about the debate in the book. A last chapter? Who could be so masochistic? Even I already wished the incident had never happened.

After it was over, the Governor met me backstage.

"What did you think?" he asked.

I pretended to think it over. "Mixed," I said at last. What could I say? *It was a bloodbath…*

"I thought it got better when we got more into the issues," the Governor said.

"True," I said loudly.

"These things always play better on TV than they do in the room," he said. I saw some doubt flickering in his eyes. Then the smile returned, but it was not quite as clear.

The election was two weeks away. I did not know at that moment that he was already planning a final surprise.

EIGHT

AFTER THE DEBATE my wife emailed me the following:

Subj:
Hazlitt on hate
Without something to hate, we should lose the very spring of thought and action… Pure good soon grows insipid, wants variety and spirit. Love turns to indifference or disgust: hatred alone is immortal.

The Governor had a different view of hate in his biography, written months before the debate:

I've always found that if you hate yourself it won't be long before others hate you too. I used to think nothing good could come of this. But never say never, and there's a time and a place for everything.

I had skipped over this paragraph the first time through. There were a lot of passages that read like that, dark ones, or ones that were slightly off kilter (if not outright deranged), that started with something interesting and dissolved into pointless cliché. I imagined the Governor typing these up in a shadowy room, a glass of whiskey at hand. They were cries in the dark, trying to express something he didn't allow himself to feel during the day. Why would I read this more than once? The near-Biblical homilies at the end choked the life out of whatever was there at the beginning.

After the debate I went back to this passage. What if it was literally his belief? That he had hated himself on purpose, knowing that others would hate him, and that something good would come out of it? Could that explain this whole decision to run? That he would bottom out, force everyone to expunge the full force of their hatred against him in a few months, and then build himself up again from that? For surely Hazlitt was wrong in at least one respect: hate would turn to indifference too. The Governor had had his turn: there would be new things to hate.

The day after the debate a poll came out. The Governor was still losing (by a lot), but his poll numbers had gone up. It was only two points—within the margin of error. Astute commentators pointed out that the three-day poll was taken mostly before the debate. But most people don't look that carefully, and the bump was enough for the Governor to spin the narrative. A surge! A comeback!

"The people have chosen forgiveness," he beamed on a live remote.

And I thought that maybe this had been part of his plan. *A time and a place for everything.*...Could he have given the people someone to hate on purpose? Had he welcomed it? Given it to us as a gift? I didn't think that he'd set out to do it—I thought his affair was either love or a midlife crisis, as everyone else did. But once he found himself in that role, had he decided to encourage it? Or at least accept it? Or at least understand?

I tried to raise this with him, but he cut me off.

"You have to come up!" he shouted over the phone. "You won't want to miss this. We have our second-to-last chapter!"

I knew he still thought his victory would be the last chapter. But the second-to-last?

"Two points in the polls?"

"Tina's back," he said.

I took the next flight to Milwaukee.

"GREEN SHOOTS!" THE GOVERNOR SAID when I saw him. He'd just wrapped up one of his "free fundraisers" in a church basement. It had been a reporter's joke—the Governor got all of his money from a handful of wealthy supporters, mostly from outside the state. He had no "fundraisers" per se—they were billed as such, but he waived the fee to try to get a few people in the audience. The Governor had tried to turn this to his advantage: Can't be bought! Voice of the people! Ideas politician! My opponent has fundraisers where she asks you for money. My fundraisers are *free*!

("I have free fundraisers too," his opponent said calmly. "They're called *events*.")

Green shoots? Six people had attended, two of them below voting age. The Governor shook their hands, talking to me as everyone waited their turn.

"I told you there were two things that could turn this thing around," he told me. "The debate and Tina." He smiled. "Well I just hit the trifecta."

I was not surprised he didn't know what a trifecta was. I was, however, surprised he considered the debate a success. Had he no access to the Internet? "Two points in a poll?" I asked.

"Every flood starts with a raindrop," he said. "And the ark wasn't built in a day. Even *God* took 40 nights to get his flood rolling."

There were so many problems with this I didn't know

where to begin, just on a pure English-language level. But I didn't want to think about that. My theory of hate-jujitsu crumbled. He didn't understand the hate. This wasn't some kind of four-dimensional chess game. He didn't welcome the hate. How could he? He craved love like any politician. He was hungry for it—hungry for the six people, wished it was six hundred, six thousand, six million.

Finally the last woman left. She was in her seventies, probably a widow either literally or effectively, and the Governor flirted with her in his expert way.

"Have you been exercising?" she asked.

"Yes, ma'am."

"I thought so," she said, batting her eyelashes. "You have a nice shape, Governor."

He chuckled. "Now ma'am, I think you're trying to get me in trouble. Did my opponent send you over here?"

She raised an eyebrow and lifted a shoulder, glowing with excitement.

He winked and lowered his voice. "You're not *Italian*, are you?"

"Governor!"

She turned, obviously delighted, and *sashayed* toward the door. The Governor shook his head, bemused. It was a moment to savor, a reminder of why he'd been a national figure for something other than embarrassment. He was an ideas man with serious retail-politician skills. It was no wonder people used to think he'd be president. Before the scandal, his lack of self-awareness had looked like a strength.

That was it for the free fundraiser. We headed for the car.

"Tina's been calling," he said as we drove to Greenfield. "She offered some advice."

"What was it?"

"She said, 'Don't talk about your heart.' She's always been a good judge of that kind of thing."

He was quiet for a moment. We drove past a Culver's.

"She's savvy, I know," he began.

As the Governor spoke, I got a sinking feeling. Apparently she called after the debate and said she was planning to give an interview. She hadn't decided yet which network—they all wanted her.

"I told her she's got to give local news something too, like a teaser, or a quick promo. We need them as much as we need the big guys. That's a good tip—is that in the book?"

"At least five times," I said.

"Let's add it," he said, ignoring me.

He was as excited as I'd ever seen him. I found it hard to believe. It was not clear to me from anything he said that Tina was as on board as he seemed to think.

"Has she told you what she's going to say?"

"I know what she'll say. *Forgiveness heals us all.* She's a good Christian. She knows I've suffered." He drummed the dashboard with his knuckles, something with more exuberance than rhythm. "Her love for me—and for the people of this state—it's too much! I'm *overwhelmed*. Love has won!"

I didn't have the heart to deflate this bubble.

"Is two weeks enough time?"

"Are you kidding? Nobody knows Paige Perkins, she has zero name recognition. Everyone knows me. They're just waiting to like me again."

I actually agreed with this in part.

"And she—what's she done? A software business? They don't get that. They get *factories* and *farms*. Factories that make things you can hold in your hand or drive around. Farms that put food on your table. She's not ready for the big leagues. I am. Say what you want about me, I'm ready. They all know that. But right now, a vote for me is a vote against Tina, and they love her. They believe her and they trust her. When she forgives me, they'll forgive me. My numbers will skyrocket. Two chops? It'll happen in two minutes."

He shook his head and pounded his leg with his fist. "This is going to be *amazing* to watch. And you're up close!" He took a breath and said, with significance:

"It's the greatest story ever told."

"Your comeback?"

"Comeback? It's a *resurrection*. A political resurrection. Maybe that should be our title. But what's great is that it's all about her—this is about my wife and the love she shows. For my sons, for our family…"

He stopped. His face was shining with tears.

"HE CALLED IT," I SAID, "a resurrection."

My wife and I were enjoying one of our conjugal phone calls. I was outside a free fundraiser, standing on the sidewalk. Nobody passed me. It was very quiet.

"He said that? With no irony?"

I smiled. He didn't have irony. It was a strange thing. He was not that much older than me and had a similar background. How had he not developed a sense of irony? My generation was steeped in it—crippled by it, you might say.

"Maybe he meant he was Lazarus. Right? Not Christ."

"He said it was the greatest story ever told."

"Oh good lord," said my wife.

My wife was as excited as anyone to hear that Tina was going to speak. At last! The beloved spouse gets her turn! Of course it would appeal to her—it would appeal to anyone.

As we talked I said I was not feeling so good about this new development, though I couldn't figure out why, exactly.

For the next fifteen minutes, as the Governor got delayed by the good folks in the donut shop, I talked through the possibilities. I admitted that I had actually come to see things his way.

He had convinced me that the interview was going to

happen, that it would happen very soon. I was not convinced that she was back on board. But who knew? She wasn't running herself. What good would it do her to endorse his opponent? If he lost, what would be in it for her and his kids? Whereas if he won—well, good things accrued to people with power, and to people with access to people with power.

And I accepted his analysis. Two weeks *was* enough time. This *was* a story of forgiveness and redemption. Maybe this *was* happening. She would forgive, the Governor would surge, and become a congressman. The madness and mania surrounding him would end.

So why was I so anxious? So filled with dread? Hadn't I been in this for the excitement? Now I wanted to fly home, crawl under the covers, and pretend I'd never met the Governor.

Maybe I'd wanted to watch him fail? I believed in failure. I believed that politics was a path I didn't take, that I'd chosen a life of quiet failure over one of sensational public disgrace.

Maybe that was it: his failure made me feel better about myself. At least I wasn't him, absorbing those blows, taking that ridicule on the chin.

Thinking this through helped me turn things around. Because as soon as I thought this, I felt a surge of excitement. I *did* want him to win. I was writing his book, I had proximity to power. His success would justify *me*, in a sense, or at least give *me* a measure of success. It would give me meaning.

"He'll win and you won't get any of that," my wife said. "It's the story of your life."

I TUNED IN ALONG WITH THE REST of the country to watch Tina Olson give her first public interview since the scandal broke. It was scheduled for an hour, in prime time. Only I was not in my living room, watching with other members of my household. I was sitting in a motel room in Racine, watching with the Governor. We sat on two chairs, one at the foot of each of the two beds, with a wastebasket stuffed with fast food wrappers.

The show started with ten minutes of clips. The snowmobiling quote, the staff who didn't know where he was, the deer-in-the-headlights interviews. Then the debate with Paige Perkins—and I was a little surprised to see how this played. It made the Governor look good, mostly by making Paige look mean.

The Governor was wearing a faint smile on his face: he could see where this was headed too. By the time the host started speaking, describing Tina, the Governor was chuckling under his breath. All the embarrassment and ridicule would soon be in his past. Part of his comeback story. His resurrection. The gods of television had decided.

They cut to the studio. The interviewer was beautiful: perfect hair, perfect makeup. Tina looked better. Radiant, more beautiful, with less effort. It was clear now that she had been watching the clips as well, on a monitor.

"Hard to watch?" asked the interviewer.

Tina smiled in a pained way. "It's not easy."

The camera cut to the interviewer. "I think most of us are sitting here thinking, if that were me, I'd hate him for what he did. I'd be out there shouting it from the rooftops, venting my anger. You never said that. Why no interviews?"

"Well, I am the mother of four sons. They come first."

"Your sons have been critical."

"They're grown men. They can make their own decisions."

"Do they love their father? Because frankly, some of their criticisms have been…"

Tina's mouth tightened into a grim smile. "They protect me. I'm not here to talk about them."

"And now he's on the verge of a comeback. Tom—the Governor—your husband—is running for Congress. A poll shows he's rebounding. Why did you choose to speak now, during the final two weeks of his campaign?"

"It's taken me a while to get to where I am."

"A critic might say you planned this to turn the race around."

Tina met the interviewer's gaze. "I think it's important for voters to know where I stand."

There was a pause. The interviewer waited patiently, then said, in the softest and gentlest of voices, "What do you want to tell the voters, Tina?"

Tina sighed. She smiled, shook her head slowly, and composed herself. When she spoke it was with clarity and confidence:

"That I hate him. And it's okay. They can hate him as well."

The interviewer seemed to be taken by surprise and made no reaction. Next to me, the Governor made a kind of rattling sound in the back of his throat.

I stared ahead, alarmed and unable to look at him. Where were his *handlers*? Where were his *supporters*? Why was it only me, witnessing this horrible event in his presence?

The interviewer reacted as you'd expect she would, all *let's talk about hate*, and *gosh that's a strong word*. She noted that it's what Paige Perkins had said as well, and does this mean we should all hate all adulterers, and so forth. I finally managed to glance at the Governor. His face looked ashen, but he was smiling, incapable of not smiling, like a ventriloquist dummy someone left at a funeral.

"Do you want me to turn it off?"

He said nothing. That horrible grin stayed attached to his face. I stood and went to the television.

"No, leave it," he said in a clotted voice, as his wife described the moment she knew it was okay to hate, that it was healthy and healing and productive to do so.

I tried to show some sympathy. "This is not what you expected…"

JACKE WILSON

The blood returned to his face. His terrible frozen smile faded. Now he looked like someone wiser, more experienced—it was now the smile of someone who had returned from hell. Whatever blows he'd taken were starting to be absorbed.

"The only thing in life to expect is the unexpected," he said. "Let's add that to the book."

It was already in there at least a dozen times.

"Absolutely," I said, and sat back down.

NINE

THE GOVERNOR DIDN'T WIN THE ELECTION. He lost in a big, humiliating, record-breaking way. I read some giddy analysis under headlines like "Worst Defeat in History?" There were entire towns he lost unanimously. He lost every conceivable demographic: lost among women, lost among men, lost among the old and the young, the poor and the wealthy. Blue collar, white collar, Christian, other, black, white, Vietnamese—everything. (White men over the age of 80 who have never voted? Lost them too!) In Lake Geneva he finished fourth behind Paige Perkins, Vince Lombardi, and "My Penis."

I tried to reach him but he didn't answer. On television I watched his surprisingly lackluster speech. I had thought he might use the forum as a chance to talk about adversity or comebacks or how the heart handles despair. But there was none of that, just mumbled thanks and a few references to the glories of the democratic process. It was as if he hadn't expected to lose, or more likely, that the Tina interview had crushed him.

After his concession speech the television cut immediately to the old reliables: the snowmobiling press conference (again!), his heart speech, the fumbling debate performance. On the other half of the screen his opponent was gushing about the victory and the People. Her speech had no word of praise for the Governor that I could detect.

I had offered to go to Wisconsin on Election Day. He had been noncommittal. Now I felt strange: maybe I should have pressed.

A week later I finally heard from him. He was planning to take some time off, he said. His voice sounded hollow and far away.

"Think about your next move?" I prompted.

He didn't respond.

I drove to the airport and flew into Madison as soon as I could.

I DON'T KNOW IF HE HAD any kind of closure in mind, or if it was all on my end, but it saddened me that he suggested we meet at the Big Boy. A circle was closing. Endings always make me sad.

The first thing I did was turn over the pages of his manuscript. They were still in the box—read but not edited.

"Oh yes," he said, recovering after the initial surprise at recognizing the materials. "That."

"I'm not going to take your money," I said. "I just—"

"I'll pay you for your time."

His smile was back. The life behind it was not as strong. Something inside him had dimmed.

I had plenty of reasons for resigning from the project. I couldn't figure out a theme. I didn't know how to organize it in a way that made sense. Failure and hatred had emerged as the organizing principles, and that didn't seem desirable, though it did seem accurate. I knew it wasn't the story of his life that he wanted to tell.

I mumbled something about the lessons being solid and we should try again when we have a better ending. He nodded, looking as if something in me had dimmed as well, and maybe it had.

"I already ate," he said. "You hungry?"

"I'm fine."

"Shrimp salad!"

I frowned with confusion.

"I mean you have to try it. Shrimp salad!"

He was tired, he looked old, but he said those words—shrimp salad!—with as much enthusiasm as he could muster. He had no wife anymore. His kids hated him. His career lay dead at the bottom of a pit. As a person, as a human being, he was completely, utterly humiliated. And I, the final straw, had just shoved at him the miserable pages of his life, which I could no longer bear to possess. Because they were pressing down on me. I felt like I'd been stuffed into a hole, a dark place, with something dark and heavy lying down on my chest. That I couldn't breathe as long as those pages were my responsibility.

There was nothing to learn. No analysis was adequate. There was just him and his shrimp salad. And his "shrimp salad!"

He ordered dessert. A big smile for the waitress.

"They work hard here," he told me, shaking his head. "Half their salary comes from tips."

He looked around at the waitstaff, the décor, whatever there was to look at. "This is such a good Wisconsin place," he observed.

A Big Boy! He said this about a Big Boy! I decided I couldn't be with the mild anymore. The meek were tearing me down, as they always had. I needed edge. And anger. I needed to shout. I needed tears and rage and howls in the night.

I said goodbye to the Governor.

He was going to fade away, and no lives would change. Not his, not mine, not ours. It would all slip away.

I walked out into the Wisconsin night, under the midnight sky, the wide-open stars. It was the time of year I

love most, football season ending, basketball season starting up. Dark buses on the highways like ships at sea, sail-
ing through the night to warm, lit gyms.

In the parking lot, the wind blew crispy leaves across
my feet.

I walked around the side of the restaurant, taking the
long way, away from my car. The sidewalk ended and I
walked on gravel, between the row of bushes and the restaurant, careful to stay in the shadows, just away from the
windows. But I glanced into the restaurant anyway. Why?
Why, why, why did I do this? I was not sure at the time.
Now I think I was trying to see what he looked like when I
wasn't there—and when he wasn't expecting me. I was
gone. What was he now?

He was in ruins, of course—I knew that he was. He
had to be. But you wouldn't know it from his appearance.

The waitress sets a plate before him. He smiles and says
something. She laughs and walks away.

He takes a bite of the cherry pie as I slink away into the
night.

And this is where I end, the only place I can. With the
last image of the Governor: just him, alone, hated by the
world. And me in the dark thinking about all the people
who love to hate. Myself included. Myself most of all.

The Governor, the man, is chewing slowly, gazing
ahead. He might be thinking about what's become of him,
brooding on how he fell from popular to despised thanks
to love or lust or whatever it actually was. Or he might be
enjoying himself, feeling good about where he is and what
he's been through and what lies ahead. He might have
nothing in mind other than the Wisconsin evening and the
warm lights of the Big Boy and the smile of the waitress.
The taste of the cherry pie, so good it has to be from Wisconsin.

And I might have insight into who he is and I might
not. All I can tell you is that it's impossible to tell.

ABOUT THE AUTHOR

JACKE WILSON is the pen name of a writer who was born and raised in Wisconsin and has since lived in Chicago, Italy, Taiwan, Michigan, Seattle, California, and New York City. Formerly a Capitol Hill staffer, he now lives and works in the Washington D.C. area. He can be found at http://www.jackewilson.com and @WriterJacke.

Printed in Great Britain
by Amazon

87864378R00058